"Molly, we have a damage control problem because of that debate you were in," her dad said. . . . "Somehow Claytie Lawson got hold of your school newspaper. He quotes you as saying that your dad's in favor of gun control."

"It's true, isn't it, Dad?" Molly asked. "You told me yourself."

"Yes, but I didn't mean you could quote me in your debate. I was giving you a private opinion. You know how careful the members of a congressman's family have to be about anything they say."

Congressman Spalding played with a letter opener on the desk. "When I run again I'll need to have a policy ready on gun control." He was quiet a moment. He added, "Or not run again."

*Would Molly be the cause of her father's defeat?*

# The Congressman's Daughter

by Patricia Maloney Markun

*For the Soup Group, a brave band of friends
who dare to counsel each other in writing books
for young people:*

Brent Ashabrenner
Caroline Levine
Claudia Mills
Brenda Seabrooke
Ellen Showell

*With profound appreciation*

Published by Willowisp Press
801 94th Avenue North, St. Petersburg, Florida 33702

Copyright © 1994 by Willowisp Press,
a division of PAGES, Inc.

Printed in the United States of America

2 4 6 8 10 9 7 5 3 1

ISBN 0-87406-674-3

# One

THREE days, Molly thought. I can't believe I've been stuck in this station wagon for three whole days trying to keep Billy and Blitzen happy so Mom can drive in peace.

Before leaving Texas for the long journey to Washington, D.C., 12-year-old Molly promised to keep her younger brother entertained and their big, brownish gray Weimaraner calm. Well, as calm as a dog can be cooped up in the back of a station wagon. Of course, Molly let 8-year-old Billy win at steal-the-pack and checkers. She played tic-tac-toe until even the thought of Xs and Os made her want to throw up. To make things worse, loose game pieces and cards had gotten stuck in the back of the car seat and now were poking her. If she only had a friend her age in the car, the long trip wouldn't be so awful.

"There it is, Molly!" Billy yelled suddenly. "The Washington Monument! Ha-ha. I saw it first!"

Molly moved over and looked out her brother's window to where he was pointing. The tall, white shaft stood high above the city, easy to see from the bridge over the Potomac River they were now crossing.

"Wow, Billy, look at that!" Molly said in awe. Lit up against the dark sky, the monument looked almost translucent.

You can almost see through it, Molly thought, as if it were made of smoky glass.

Mrs. Spalding had been to Washington only a few times before, but she drove like an expert through the unfamiliar city that was now their new home. "We're on Pennsylvania Avenue, kids," Mom called out a few minutes later. "Look over there at the end of the street."

Molly leaned forward and looked over her mother's shoulder down the long, wide avenue. High on a hill at the very end stood the Capitol. Molly recognized its famous white marble dome with the statue of a lady on top. How beautiful, Molly thought. To think that her Dad was going to be Congressman Justin Spalding and work in that very building! Molly never realized how enormous the shining building was until her mom drove alongside it up Capitol Hill.

"We're looking for 300 C Street Southeast," Mrs. Spalding said. "That's our new address."

"That's A Street Southeast," Molly said, reading a well-lighted street sign as her mother slowed the car.

"Two more blocks then," her mother said. She turned on C Street. "Can you see any numbers on the houses, or is it too dark?"

"Two—five—five," Billy called out.

Molly felt prickles on the back of her neck. The house Dad bought for them when he left Texas a few weeks ago must be near here. What would it look like? Just then she saw bright brass numbers on a house. "Three hundred!" she cried. "That's it!"

She looked beyond the numbers to the house itself. What a neat house Dad had picked out. Mrs. Spalding drove into the driveway, and they looked in silence at their new home, which was lit by the street light nearby. The house was brick with lots of shutters. A round tower on one side of the house fit neatly into one corner of the triangular lot that was surrounded by a wrought-iron fence.

"Hey, I like it," Billy said. "Three stories. And there's even a fence for Blitzen." He turned and petted the big Weimaraner. The dog's wet nose was pressed up against the back window of the station wagon.

"I think I like it, too," their mom said cheerfully. "We're going to have some great times in this house."

"There's a light on in the living room," Molly said. "Dad must be waiting for us inside. I guess he didn't hear the car." She opened the door. "Let's go see."

Together they opened the old-fashioned, wrought-iron gate, and walked up broad stone steps to an ornate doorway. Molly grabbed the large brass knocker and banged it against the door three times.

"That should wake Dad up!" Billy giggled.

They waited impatiently in the cold, dark night. After a minute or so, Billy gave the door another three whacks with the knocker.

Where was Dad? Molly wondered. Could they possibly have the wrong address? She spied an open space between the heavy drapes covering the front window and peeked in.

"I see one of our lamps. This is the right house," Molly reported. Billy peeked in too, seeing, as Molly had, their brass floor lamp with its familiar scalloped turquoise shade.

Billy turned to their mother and said, "This must be our house, Mom. Our lamp's inside. I guess the movers got here before we did."

The cold winter wind swept over them. Molly shivered. Her thin Texas sweater wasn't warm enough for this climate. She wished they were already settled in their new home, warm and comfortable, with all their own things that were still waiting beyond that locked door. Where was Dad?

"Can we force the door open, Mom?" Molly asked. "Remember we did that once in Spring Grove when we got back from vacation and couldn't find the key?"

"Not in this house," Mom explained. "Molly, look at that little sign in the window," her mother said. "Those words

'Minute Man Security System' mean this house is protected by a burglar alarm. If we tried to break in, you'd hear a siren, and the police would come. And we'd have a hard time explaining what we were doing here."

Molly heard a click. She looked around and saw a tall, familiar figure opening the gate.

"Joan, Molly, Billy! Hi!" Dad ran up the stairs and crushed them to his chest in one big bear hug.

From the station wagon came Blitzen's welcoming bark. Dad was his special favorite.

"I sure am sorry to be late. I was called to the Capitol for a special meeting, but I was hoping I'd be back before you got here."

He pulled a brass key out of his pocket and swung open the heavy door. He put his arm around his wife, and the family walked into their new home together.

"I hope you'll like the house, Joan," he said. He flicked on a switch to the elegant chandelier hanging high above the entrance hallway.

Then Dad moved quickly to the nearest wall and punched three buttons on a panel.

"That turns off the security system," he explained. "I don't want to frighten you, but you're in the big city now. You're all going to have to learn to work the burglar alarm. When you come home, you have 30 seconds to close the door and put in our secret code before the alarm goes off. Our code is the date of your mother's and my wedding anniversary, May 23, so the code numbers are 5-2-3. Now I want you to try it."

They gathered around the metal panel and each one practiced punching the numbers.

"Spring Grove, Texas was never like this!" Mom said.

"I'll get Blitzen," Billy volunteered. He ran down the stairs and opened the station wagon door. The big dog rushed headlong into the house to join the family. Dad closed the door firmly and locked it from the inside.

"Okay, now let me show you the rest of the house. You kids probably want to see your bedrooms first," Dad said. "Billy, you're on the second floor at the top of the stairs. Molly, you're up on the third floor. Your Mom and I thought you'd like to be up there by yourself. Wait until you see the view of the city you have from your room, Molly!"

Molly eagerly ran upstairs to search for her room. Their house in Texas was ranch style with all the rooms on one floor. She'd always wanted a room up above everybody else's—just like Jo in one of her favorite books, *Little Women.*

On the second floor she caught a glimpse of a narrow stairway at the far end of the hall. She hurried up those smaller stairs to the third floor. In the dim light coming through an open door at the end of a short hall, she could see her white French provincial bed. She felt for the wall switch and turned on the light.

It was a round room, with a ceiling that came to a peak. Molly felt almost as if she were inside a large white ice cream cone. Her furniture had been arranged neatly in the round space. What a marvelous room! She realized she must be in the top of the tower they had seen from the street.

Windows went around the room, and she ran from window to window trying to see all she could of the city.

Suddenly she stopped. Through the window behind her desk she could see the dome—the massive lighted dome of the Capitol—only a few blocks away. It stood silent and majestic, glowing pearly white against the night sky. She could hardly believe the scene was real and not some picture on a poster. Molly thought about how she had seen reporters on TV stand on the Capitol steps in front of the dome to report from Washington. And now she had her own private view right here from her upstairs bedroom.

I'm lucky to be a congressman's daughter, she thought. It's going to be great living in the middle of Washington, D.C. Molly knew her life here was going to be a lot different from what it had been in Spring Grove where her mom and dad had been small-town lawyers.

Wouldn't her seventh grade gang from Spring Grove Middle School love to be here in this room! Eve and Sybil and Leslie and Grace. Most of all, her best friend, Brooke. She imagined each one of them here now, lying on the bed or on the floor playing CDs, talking about rock stars, and eating brownies they had made.

She sat down at her desk, took out a

piece of her special lilac stationery, and quickly wrote the first line of a letter to Brooke.

"Dear Brooke, I'm looking out the window of my new bedroom in Washington, and guess what I can see!"

Her pen stopped moving. She imagined Brooke reading the letter to the other girls in the lunchroom at school. She looked up at the dome without seeing it. Then a disturbing thought struck her. She had no friends here at all. Not one. Tears clouded her eyes. She wiped them away and went on with her letter.

# Two

MOLLY woke up early. What motel are we in now? she wondered. She looked up and saw the round ceiling that went up to a point. Then she remembered. She was in her new bedroom, and this morning was the swearing-in ceremony for the members of Congress.

"School can wait one day," her dad had said last night. "I want you and Billy to be there when I'm sworn in as a congressman. I hope it's a day you will always remember."

She took a shower and put on the turquoise velvet dress her mother had rescued from a suitcase and ironed for her. It was hard to believe that only a few weeks ago she'd worn this dress to the school

15

Christmas party. She slid into her black patent leather pumps and made a face remembering how she and her mother had argued about the shoes in the store. The heels weren't as high as she would have liked, but then again, her mother still thought she was a baby. So they had compromised.

One thing hasn't changed, she thought, as she looked into her dressing table mirror. I still have the same awful hair I had back in Spring Grove.

"Just like your father's beautiful, thick hair," her grandmother always said. Dad's hair looked great. Hers was long and wild and bushy. Just plain old mousy brown. She brushed it furiously.

Molly pulled up the shades and looked out to see the neighborhood by daylight. All the houses were red brick, not wood, the way they were in Spring Grove. Her eyes caught sight of a big moving van pulling up at the house next door. A girl came out of the house, walked to the cab of the truck, and spoke to the driver.

Molly leaned closer to the window to see better. The girl had long black hair, and she looked as though she were about the same age as Molly. Was a 12-year-old moving in next door? What good luck that would be! Molly put on her coat and hurried downstairs. No one else was up yet. She turned off the alarm and opened the door hesitantly, half expecting a siren to go off, and went outside.

The girl was walking back toward her house. Before she could go inside, Molly ran up to meet her.

"Hi, I'm Molly Spalding," she said. "We just moved in, too. I guess we're going to be next-door neighbors."

"Vivian! Vivian!" A woman called out in a no-nonsense voice. "Come on in. We leave for the plane in ten minutes!"

Molly drew in her breath, disappointed. The girl was moving away, not moving in. "I'm sorry," Vivian said, as she turned to leave. "I mustn't be late."

"Please tell me," Molly called after her. "Did you—did you like living here?"

The girl looked back at her with sad eyes. "I love Washington. I hate to leave. Have you heard about Potomac fever, yet? Don't get it. Bye."

And then she was gone.

Molly wondered what kind of disease Potomac fever was. It must be awful, because that girl looked terribly unhappy. Bad luck for me she's moving, Molly thought. It would have been neat to have a girl her own age right next door. And Vivian seemed friendly, too.

Molly walked back to her house, where she and her family spent the morning getting ready for the big event. Congressman Spalding had polished his shoes until they shined. He called them his lucky shoes because his wife had bought them for him when he decided to run for office.

Soon they were walking into the Capitol with other House members and their families.

"Good morning, Congressman!"

"Welcome to Washington, Congressman!"

The guards at the Capitol door welcomed Molly's dad as if they were old friends.

All around them Molly could see other new representatives and their families. A few kids looked her age. I wonder if I'll ever meet them, she thought.

As the line moved forward, Mrs. Spalding whispered to Molly and Billy, "The newspaper and television reporters are waiting for us." She nodded her head in the direction of a cluster of men and women with cameras and notebooks a few feet away. "One of them could be from Texas, so smile as we go by. At least don't stick out your tongues at a TV camera."

"Oh, Mom!" Molly protested. "Do you think we're morons?"

A tall, lean man with a black camera case bobbing on his hip left the press group and walked quickly toward the Spaldings.

"Congratulations, Justin!" he called out. "I haven't seen you since the election."

"Howdy, Claytie!" Dad shook the man's hand enthusiastically. Then he turned to his wife. "Joan, you remember Clayton Lawson from the *Spring Grove Sentinel.*"

Molly gasped. This man was Clayton Lawson? She'd never met him, but she had read the news stories he wrote about her Dad during the campaign—stories full of lies. How could Dad even talk to him? And shake his hand?

" . . . and our children Molly and Billy."

Molly only caught her father's last words and found herself shaking hands with the reporter, too. She expected his hand to be cold and clammy, but it was warm, and his handshake was firm. He smiled at her as if they were old friends from home. Molly couldn't force herself to smile. Her jaw seemed to be stuck and her mouth wouldn't open.

"I've moved here, too, Justin," Mr. Lawson said. "I'm going to cover the Congress for ten Texas newspapers. Watch for my new column, 'Texans on Capitol Hill.'"

"Congratulations, Claytie," Dad said. He added, "I'm the newest of the twenty-six representatives from Texas, so I'm probably the least newsworthy of them all. You won't have much to report about me for a while."

"Who knows?" Mr. Lawson grinned as if all kinds of news could happen. "You might be appointed to an important committee that's full of excitement. How about a picture of the Spalding family for the folks back home? Smile, Molly," he said, peering through the lens of his camera. "This is supposed to be a happy day for you."

Clayton Lawson looked at each of the four Spaldings through his lens as if he were memorizing them for a future article. Then, after taking several photos, he turned and hurried back to rejoin the media group.

"Mom," Molly whispered as the line inched forward, "is that the same man who wrote those awful articles about Dad during the campaign?"

"The very one," she replied.

"Then why were you so nice to him, Dad?" Molly asked.

He sighed. "Politics, Molly. I beat the candidate Claytie was supporting, and I have to be a good sport. Besides, we have to be careful how we deal with the press, because they always have the last word." He looked directly at Molly and added quietly, "Remember, you are a congressman's daughter. The media are watching you. Anything unusual any of us do could be called 'news.'"

"Justin, you'll scare her to death," Molly's mother said. She put her arm around her daughter and hugged her. "Remember this, hon. Don't talk to strangers and don't talk to the press."

As Molly walked past the mob of photographers and reporters, she thought of them as a pack of lions in the circus, facing "Molly Spalding, Lion Tamer." She looked right at them, inhaled deeply, and smiled broadly into their big round lenses.

In her head she composed a line that Mr. Lawson could use with the photos he snapped. "THE HAPPY SPALDING FAMILY ON THEIR WAY TO THE SWEARING-IN CEREMONY." From the stories he wrote about Dad in the past, she was sure he'd never write anything that nice. The Spaldings were ushered into the House of Representatives and took their places on the blue velvet seats. Molly looked up at the high blue ceiling decorated with gold. In front of them stood the imposing desk of the Speaker of the House.

"Members sit here when the House is in session," Dad explained. "This is the only time in our two-year term that our families can join us here." He grinned. "So enjoy your seats."

Bang. Bang. Bang. The sound of the Speaker's gavel signaled the beginning of the new session. The names of the new members were called out one by one, and each man or woman walked to the front to be sworn in.

"Justin Bryce Spalding from the State of Texas!" The new congressman stood up, smiled at his family, and went forward to join the other men and women gathered in front of the Speaker's desk. The Chaplain of the House came forward and signaled the audience to stand. The candidates raised their right hands and promised to "defend and protect the Constitution of the United States."

A short silence followed. Then loud applause broke out. Molly found herself clapping so hard that her hands hurt. Dad worked so hard during his campaign, she thought. All those speeches. All that work for Mom and Dad to close their law office after he won the election. Worst of all had been the telephone. It rang nearly nonstop from the time Dad announced he was going to run until the morning they left Spring Grove. At last he was a Member of Congress!

Molly was so proud of him. She felt tears in her eyes. As Molly applauded, she looked over at her mother, who was still clapping.

Her eyes were wet, too.

Dad smiled broadly as he walked up the aisle.

"Congratulations, Congressman Spalding!" his wife said, and they all kissed him.

"Now we're going to a party in my new office that some friends are giving," the new congressman said. "We'll take the train to the Cannon Building. Come on." He led the way out of the Chamber.

"Train? What train?" Billy asked Molly as they hurried down the hall after their parents.

"He's teasing," Molly reassured him as they got into an elevator marked "Members Only." The elevator went down, and when the doors opened, the family was in the basement. Molly saw a network of narrow-gauge train tracks. A small train pulling five cars came into sight.

"Boy, way to go!" Billy said loudly. "See, Molly, there is a train."

He was the first one to climb into one of the four-passenger cars. The other Spaldings took their seats, filling one car. Other families got aboard. The uniformed engineer sounded a warning and the train began to move quickly through a well-lighted tunnel. The first stop was at a sign that said "Cannon Office Building," and they got out.

Dad led them through a honeycomb of halls and rooms, brass-doored elevators, and marble stairs. As they passed one office after another, Molly could see party preparations set up through the open doors.

"Every member has a party on the first day of a new session," Dad explained. "We'll be having ourselves a good old time in #4222, too."

Sure enough, a big sign propped on a stand at the doorway to his office read "CONGRATULATIONS, CONGRESSMAN SPALDING!" Next to it stood a huge bouquet of yellow Texas roses.

As the Spaldings walked through the door, Molly saw the Spring Grove postmaster with an accordion strapped over his shoulders and his hands ready and waiting, eager to play.

"The eyes of Texas are upon you!" sang the excited crowd who had gathered to welcome their new congressman. His secretary came over to Mrs. Spalding and pinned a corsage of yellow roses on her and a single yellow rose on Molly.

Handshaking started as if the campaign were beginning all over again. But these were the Spaldings' best friends, the ones who worked hardest during the election.

Imagine coming all the way from Texas just for the swearing-in, Molly thought.

"Cold shrimp and that yucky caviar!" Billy complained loudly when it was time to help themselves to the lunch at the buffet table. "Why don't they have barbecue and chili?" He lifted the silver covers off three casseroles and frowned at the contents of all of them.

Molly looked up and saw Clayton Lawson listening to Billy. I'll bet he's taking in all Billy's complaints, Molly thought. She could see the next headline on Mr. Lawson's column: "YOUNG WILLIAM SPALDING COMPLAINS ABOUT FOOD SERVED BY SPRING GROVE FRIENDS."

She had a funny feeling in the pit of her stomach. Billy could harm Dad's reputation. How could she keep him quiet?

# *Three*

MOLLY quickly went over to her brother, grabbed his arm firmly, and steered him to the other end of the table.

"Hush up, Billy," Molly whispered sharply in his ear. "That's Claytie Lawson, the newspaper reporter, over there, and he doesn't like Dad. He heard you, and he might put it in ten newspapers that you didn't like the food Dad's supporters served at this party."

"Okay, okay," he whispered back. "But I'm still not going to eat that junk." Something across the room caught Billy's attention. "There's someone my age," he said.

Molly turned and saw a boy about Billy's size standing on the other side of the buffet table inspecting the food. He was wearing a navy blue sport coat and looking even more dressed up than Billy was in his tan corduroy jacket. I bet he's another congressman's son, Molly figured.

"I'm going to talk to him," Billy said.

"Don't wander off, you hear," Molly warned him.

Billy nodded absently and slid through the crowd to reach the other boy. Molly couldn't blame him. It was the first boy his age he'd been able to talk to since they left Spring Grove four days ago.

Molly was reaching over to dunk some shrimp into a red sauce when she heard a voice beside her say, "I'll bet you're Molly."

She looked up to see a tall, redheaded woman smiling at her. "I'm Charlotte Frauenheim, your father's new press officer. How do you like Washington?"

"We only got here last night," Molly said, "but I think it's just fine so far. One thing I really like is that I can see the Capitol dome from my bedroom window."

Charlotte nodded. "I know what you mean. It is a pretty impressive sight."

Charlotte seemed interested in hearing

about their long drive from Texas and about Molly's friends in Spring Grove, even about her best friend Brooke. She was easy to talk to, Molly found. Suddenly she remembered Billy.

"Oh, excuse me, Ma'am. I'm supposed to be watching my little brother. I'll have to find him."

Molly pushed her way through the crowd, looking everywhere, even under the buffet table. No Billy. Her parents were surrounded by well-wishers, so there was no use asking them. Had Billy left the office?

Now she imagined another headline in Mr. Lawson's column: "CARELESS CONGRESSMAN LOSES SON AT SWEARING-IN PARTY."

Molly looked around quickly to find Clayton Lawson, and saw that he was busy talking to Charlotte now. She walked out of the office as slowly as she could, then ran down the hall, surprising people by looking into the doors of every office on the fourth floor. She had to find Billy.

Molly started to get angry. That Billy! She had told him not to leave the office. Where could he have gone? Probably he was with that boy in the navy blue jacket.

She passed a wide, gray marble staircase. Maybe the boys had gone down to the floor below. She hurried down the stairs and started going from room to room again. Everyone seemed to be partying. She heard the sound of Hawaiian music coming out of one office and something told her to check that one. She walked through a doorway decorated with clusters of white orchids in honor of a new representative from Hawaii, she supposed. Molly went inside and excused herself as she walked past a man in a bright print shirt who was playing a Hawaiian guitar.

At the table, which was piled high with food surrounding a centerpiece of pineapples, stood two small boys. They seemed lost among the adults who leaned over them to reach the platters on the table. The boys, each with a colorful plastic lei around his neck, were chewing contentedly.

Molly mumbled excuses and pushed through the laughing crowd. "Billy!" The whispered word shot out like a bullet as she grabbed her little brother by the coat sleeve. "You! Come with me."

She pulled him along. At the same moment, she saw a dark-haired boy about her age reach out for the other little visitor. They arrived at the door at the same time, pulling the boys along behind them. Molly got even angrier when she saw the two little boys smile and wink at each other as they were being dragged down the hall.

The older boy spoke up, "My brother Freddie always manages to find the best party in the Cannon Building. Of course I get the job of trying to find him. I'm Mark Hathaway."

"I'm Molly Spalding," she supplied. Your brother and Billy, here, met at my father's party," Molly explained. "I was supposed to be watching Billy, but they both disappeared, just like that."

Mark laughed, and she didn't feel so angry any more. "Freddie is great at disappearing. When I was his age, I was so shy at these parties I used to hide under the tablecloth. Not this kid."

All at once it seemed funny, and he and Molly laughed together. At the staircase Molly started up the stairs with Billy. Mark and his brother Freddie kept walking ahead on the third floor.

"Well—good-bye!" Molly called down awkwardly. She had assumed that the boys were going up to the fourth floor, too. "Good-bye, Freddie," Billy called loudly. "See ya," Freddie said, grinning.

Mark looked up and smiled at Molly. He waved to her briefly.

As she walked away holding Billy's arm, she realized that she hadn't had time to find out which state Mark's father or mother represented in Congress. Worst of all she hadn't really had any time to talk to him. He must be about her age, she figured.

Too late now. She was so annoyed that she hadn't learned more about him that she yanked Billy's arm even harder. "You're pulling my arm out of the socket!" he whimpered.

Good, Molly thought. You deserve it.

Outside her father's office, she pulled off the orange plastic lei from around Billy's neck and pushed it into his jacket pocket.

"If Mr. Lawson is still there, don't tell him you ran off to a party somewhere else," she warned him, brushing some crumbs off his collar and slicking back his hair.

By now the guests were leaving. Clayton Lawson was still talking to Charlotte and writing in a notebook. Maybe this time he'd say something good about Dad in his column, Molly hoped.

"Thanks for finding Billy," Mom whispered in Molly's ear, before turning to bid farewell to the mayor of Spring Grove. Her dad was thanking each friend for coming to the party and bidding everyone farewell, joking with all of them as they went out the door. Molly saw joy radiating in his smile and his triumph made her happy too.

It's Dad's greatest day, Molly thought.

Somehow, now that he was a congressman he seemed like a different person. She realized all of sudden that her dad now had several hundred thousand people from their part of Texas to look out for. He was a public figure, not just a small-town lawyer looking after his family.

A feeling of uneasiness, even fear, swept over Molly as she said good-bye over and over again to their friends from Texas.

Today my dad's officially in the House, and I've lost a part of him, Molly thought. Lots of other Texans will be getting a share of him along with us.

The thought didn't comfort her.

# *Four*

"**Y**OU'RE going to love my old school, Molly," Dad said at breakfast the next morning. "In some ways the years I spent at Shipton while your grandpa was working in Washington were the happiest times of my life."

Molly smiled and nodded but said nothing. Dad didn't enter in the middle of the school year, Molly thought, the way I am. It's always harder in January. I wonder if it's an easy school.

Mom came in then, looking relieved. She had just returned from taking Billy to his new school a few blocks away.

"It seems like a happy little school," she reported. "I think he'll find friends there."

Mom checked her watch. "We'd better leave now for Shipton."

As they drove through Washington, Molly thought of her class at Spring Grove Middle School. She'd gone to school in that little town all her life, so she knew almost everyone. Last September she'd been elected class president, and some days she had felt as though she almost ran the seventh grade. That was all over now.

Mom turned the station wagon into a driveway near a small sign that said "THE SHIPTON FRIENDS SCHOOL" and parked in a visitor's space. The way Dad talked, Molly thought, the school would be almost as big as the Capitol and surrounded with pillars like the Lincoln Memorial. Instead, there were just a few plain red brick buildings set into a hillside with some tennis courts nearby.

"This school is run by the Quakers, Molly," her mom explained as they walked up the sidewalk to the entrance. "Their real name is the Society of Friends. That's why it's called Shipton Friends School. A long time ago Quakers were called 'the plain people.' Notice that the school is rather plain looking, too. Quakers don't spend money on fancy architecture."

As they walked up the stairs she added, "The Quakers used to dress in plain black clothing—no colors allowed."

A picture came into Molly's head of the man with the funny hat on the oatmeal box. What if she had to wear a long black uniform? Dad hadn't mentioned that, but she knew she'd hate it.

"Good morning, ma'am." A boy who had just come out the front door smiled, and held the door open for them. He looked friendly. Molly smiled at him, because she was happy to see that he was wearing a red-and-white sweater and blue corduroy pants. No plain black uniform or big brimmed hat either.

Inside the door a prominent sign pointed the way to the headmaster's office. The very sound of the word made Molly's insides tighten.

But Headmaster Chipman turned out to be a kind-looking man with a soft voice. He greeted them as if it were his most important job of the day and urged them to sit down. Then he reached for a file with the name "MARY SPALDING" printed on it in large letters.

"I was happy to get this good record from your Texas school," he said. "We have only one midyear opening in the seventh grade, and we do give preference to children of Shipton graduates. That is, if we feel they can measure up to our academic standards. Your record shows you can. Welcome to Shipton Friends." He stood. "Let's go meet your homeroom teacher, Mrs. Gale."

The headmaster led them down a long hall and up some stairs, stopping at 7C. Here it comes, Molly thought, a room full of strange faces to stare at me.

Headmaster Chipman knocked on the door of 7C. A smiling, white-haired lady, not quite as tall as Molly, opened it and walked into the hall, shutting the door behind her.

"So, this must be Mary Spalding," she said, before the headmaster could introduce them.

"Please, ma'am, call me 'Molly.'"

"Thank you for telling me, Molly. It's important to get a name right from the beginning."

Molly liked Mrs. Gale immediately for

being so understanding. Last year a teacher who didn't like nicknames called her Mary all year. She hated it.

The headmaster excused himself, and Mrs. Spalding asked the teacher what time she should come for Molly each day. "Molly certainly can't walk home from here," she said.

"We have two other students in this room who live on Capitol Hill, Mark Hathaway and Jocelyn Walsh," Mrs. Gale said, looking at Molly's records. "I think Jocelyn has lacrosse practice after school, but let me see about Mark. Maybe he can show Molly how to get home on the subway."

Mrs. Gale opened the door to her classroom and said, "Mark, would you please come out here for a minute?"

A boy in a gray and gold striped sweater came out of the room. Molly recognized him at once. He was the guy she had met yesterday.

"Mrs. Spalding and Molly, this is Mark Hathaway. He lives on Capitol Hill, too."

Mark grinned. "We kind of met yesterday, Mrs. Gale. At the House swearing-in ceremony."

"Our little brothers disappeared together,

and we met when we were looking for them," Molly explained. Today that incident seemed funny, and Mrs. Gale laughed as they described finding the boys at the Hawaiian party, leis and all.

"I'll meet you after school and show you how to use the subway," Mark said. "When you know how, it's easy."

Molly shivered a little as Mrs. Gale opened the door and led her inside. Now everyone would stare at her. But, including Mark, there were only five students in the room. It wasn't bad at all when Mrs. Gale said, "This is Molly Spalding, our new class member. She moved here from Texas."

She turned to Molly. "Twelve students from the class went to the library this period. These five preferred to do their homework here. There are eighteen in the class, now that you're here. Let's see about books and get you started."

By the time the rest of the class came back, Molly was seated in her favorite place—near the front on the window side of the room. No one stared at her, something she had been dreading for weeks.

When she needed a pencil, the girl across

the aisle from her gave her one and whispered, "I'm Ashley Magnuson. Welcome to Shipton."

Molly turned her attention to the front of the room. Mrs. Gale, who was also the math teacher, began to write on the chalkboard.

What's going on? Molly wondered. This isn't the kind of math we had in Spring Grove. I can't understand it. It's like listening to a foreign language.

Then Mrs. Gale wrote a problem on the board for the class to solve. While they were working, she walked over to Molly.

"I see from your records that your Texas school doesn't teach algebra in the seventh grade. Don't worry," she said quietly. "We can get a tutor for you, and you'll catch up soon enough."

For their next class, the 7C students walked down the hall to Mr. Templeton's room for language arts.

After he welcomed Molly, he said, "We are going to review some grammar today. I want a few of you to go to the chalkboard and write this sentence: 'My aunt and I went to pick daisies in the pasture.' Molly, why don't you join this group."

Molly walked hesitantly to the board, wrote the sentence in her best handwriting and waited for further directions.

"Now," said Mr. Templeton, "I want you to diagram the sentence."

Diagramming? What's that? Molly wondered. She watched the other four students at the board draw a line from various words in the sentence, write the word on the line and then label each word as a noun, verb, adjective, adverb, or conjunction. She'd learned about nouns, verbs, and other parts of speech in her school in Texas, but she knew nothing about diagramming.

Seeing her puzzled look, Mr. Templeton walked over to her and said, "Don't worry, Molly, we'll help you learn the things that weren't taught in your old school. You may need a tutor for a while, though."

Molly's cheeks burned as she sat down. She hated to admit it, but she knew now that in some areas this school was far ahead of Spring Grove. Maybe she wouldn't be able to learn them all quickly enough. She wondered what would happen then.

When Molly returned to her homeroom,

Mrs. Gale gave her a ticket for the lunchroom that said Table 15. When Molly found her table in the lunchroom she saw a teacher in a dark red-and-white Shipton Friends T-shirt and gym shorts seated at one head. Molly, always aware of other people's hair, noticed that she had beautiful blond hair that hung down her back in a long braid.

"Welcome to Shipton Friends," she said. "We've been expecting you. I'm Ms. Dickens, the hockey coach. Do you play hockey?"

"No," Molly admitted. "I'm from Texas, and where we live it's too warm for many winter sports. Some of the bigger cities have ice rinks, but we didn't have one in Spring Grove, so I never learned to skate or to play hockey."

The students at the table giggled, and Ms. Dickens said, "We play field hockey here—not ice hockey. But of course there was no way you could have known that."

The students at the table rattled off their names, but Molly couldn't remember most of them a minute later. She did recognize the tall girl with long golden hair who was sitting next to her. Molly remembered that she was Jocelyn Walsh, the girl from her homeroom who also lived on Capitol Hill. Jocelyn looked up, smiled, then said, "You took Vivian Keegan's place."

"Did I?" Molly answered, wondering if she should apologize. "What happened to her?"

"She was a congressman's daughter, too. Mark says that you are. She lived on the Hill not far from me. Her father lost the election in November. Lost out on gun control. She was a Shipton lifer. Mark and I are, too."

"Oh-h-h," said Molly, trying to sound interested, but she didn't understand most of what Jocelyn was saying. What was "The Hill"? Why was Vivian Keegan a "lifer"? Certainly, it had nothing to do with being a lifer in jail. But what did it mean?

Suddenly Molly remembered the girl next door who had greeted the driver of the moving van. Her mother had called her Vivian. Molly wondered if she was the same Vivian whose father lost the election.

There's so much to learn—so much about life here that I don't understand, Molly thought. I don't see how I'll ever learn it all. Well, I can't worry about it now. It's almost time for social studies.

As soon as the class began, Mr. Wolff introduced Molly to the class. Then he said, "Today is Wednesday. That means it's the day for individual reports about different countries. Adrien, the next fifteen minutes are all yours."

Mr. Wolff sat down in the back of the room, and Adrien, an African-American student, set up a slide projector, and brought papers and other items up to Mr. Wolff's desk. He set things up calmly, then began to talk.

"I lived in Kenya for three years while my father was the United States Ambassador there, so I chose that country for my report. Let me take you on a visit to Kenya. . . ."

Molly had never heard a school report like this one. Adrien had gone to school in Kenya. He had seen giraffes and lions in the wild and had observed African birds.

Adrien told about climbing halfway up Mount Kilimanjaro and of a river trip to Victoria Falls. He showed slides of his friends in Kenya and of other unique places he had visited. He even brought out a little flag of Kenya and waved it as he finished his report.

"Very well done, Adrien," Mr. Wolff said as the boy sat down. "Exactly the fifteen minutes you were allotted but jam-packed with lots of good information." He marked his grade book and then turned to Molly.

"Molly, your report won't be due until March 29. That gives you two and a half months to work on it. I'll give you a list of the countries that have been chosen already, so you don't duplicate them. You must do all the research yourself. If you have never been to the country you choose, you'll just have to do more library research."

Mr. Wolff walked to the front of the room. "Time now for current events." The class began talking about national and world news that had been in the morning newspapers. Molly hardly ever read the front page of the paper—just the comics. She felt lost again.

Two students talked about problems on the island of Cyprus. They said their fathers worked in the State Department. Where was Cyprus? Molly wondered. One of the boys had even been there and knew the island well.

"What's going on in Congress this week?"

Mr. Wolff asked, and Jocelyn and Mark both raised their hands, competing to be called on first. Molly hadn't paid attention when her parents talked about legislation at the dinner table. Apparently in this school you had to know these things. She had so much catching up to do!

Later, after school, Mark met Molly at the door to the social studies room. "I'll show you how our subway system works," he said.

As they walked to the subway station, Mark asked, "So, how do you like Shipton so far?"

"It's great," Molly answered. "Really cool." She wasn't about to tell Mark how confused she felt and that she didn't know if she would ever learn all the new things she needed to know.

They walked a few blocks to a little building with a black and white sign out in front that said METRO. Molly gasped when she caught sight of two exceptionally long, shining escalators that plunged underground almost as far as she could see.

She hoped Mark didn't notice her cringe as she stood at the top of the escalator, afraid to put her foot on the moving steps. He walked ahead and called back over his shoulder, "Come on!"

She had to follow him. She hadn't told him she was scared of heights. Although she had been on escalators in stores in some of the bigger cities in Texas, Molly had never seen one like this before. She put out a foot timidly, and felt as though she were moving to the center of the earth. She couldn't even see the bottom. Mark turned around and called up to her, "Don't worry, you'll get used to it!"

Get used to it. People kept telling her that about everything in Washington, but right now Molly didn't think she'd ever get used to it. She might spend the rest of her life just trying to get to the bottom of this gigantic escalator. She grabbed the moving, rubber-covered rails on either side and hung on for dear life. Finally she reached the bottom and ran off the escalator, happy to be on solid ground again.

Mark led her over to the ticket machine and showed her how to buy a ticket for the subway. After a short wait on the platform, a sleek silver train came along. The doors opened with a quiet swish, and Molly and Mark followed the crowd in and sat down.

After her scary escalator ride, Molly decided it was time to tell Mark the truth. "Everything's so different at Shipton from my Texas school," she admitted. "I don't see how I'll learn it all."

"You'll do it," Mark said. "This school is pretty advanced, and it takes a while."

"It's easy for you to say that," Molly replied. "How long have you been going to Shipton?"

Mark paused. "Well, I must admit I'm a lifer."

That word again! At last she would find out its meaning.

"And what's a lifer?"

"Someone who started Shipton Friends at the age of three, in pre-kindergarten. I've been going there all my life. My dad's been in Congress for six terms—twelve years. If he lost an election the way Vivian Keegan's Dad did, I'd hate to go back to Tennessee. I've been to our house there for short stays, but I've never really lived there. Dad won again in November, so we can relax for two more years."

"I talked to Vivian for a minute before they left the other day," Molly admitted.

"She told me she had Potomac fever and warned me not to get it. Is it some kind of local disease? Like Rocky Mountain spotted fever or Lyme disease?"

Mark laughed. "No, it won't kill you. Potomac fever means liking Washington so much that you don't want to leave. Vivian never lived much in South Dakota either. She was a lifer like me." Mark looked at Molly directly. "I guess I have Potomac fever, too. Being a congressman's kid is the best deal in this country. I love being right here in Washington where so much is going on. Well, there's one job that's better."

"What's that?"

"To have a father or a mother who's a senator—like Jocelyn's dad. He has to run only every six years."

"Something else," Molly said. Pent-up questions from her first day at a new school kept springing to mind. "What exactly is gun control? I've heard about it on the TV news, but I don't really understand what's involved. Jocelyn said that Vivian's dad lost the election on gun control."

Mark looked at her incredulously. "You really are from the boonies, aren't you? Gun control is a big issue here. Every few years someone in Congress tries to put through laws controlling how guns are sold. You know, like those cheap pistols they call 'Saturday Night Specials' and the more powerful stuff, like machine guns, that no one should be using outside the military. There was a dirty campaign in South Dakota about gun control, and Vivian's dad was defeated, after twenty years on the Hill, too. Everyone was shocked."

Mark got up suddenly. "Here's our stop."

Molly scrambled to gather up her books. She followed Mark's lead and headed out the doors and up a short escalator.

Mark turned around and grinned as he pointed to another giant escalator up ahead. This one seemed to be going up to the sky, but Molly could see daylight up at the end of it, and she didn't mind it so much this time.

At street level, Mark walked with Molly for a few blocks before turning off to go to his house. He told her how to get to her new home, which was three streets away.

"Tomorrow morning, if you get on the subway at 7:20 right where we got out today, you'll get to Shipton in time for

Meeting. School starts with a half-hour Meeting in the auditorium every morning."

"A meeting about what?"

"It's a Quaker Meeting. Everyone sits in silence. That's how Quakers start the day. You can pray or you can sit there and make lists in your head. Sometimes the Quakers, or some others, feel moved to speak out. But don't whisper. It's the number one rule at Shipton Friends—keep quiet during Meeting. Got it?" He smiled and turned up his street. "Well, I'm glad to be rid of you now." He grinned and walked off.

Molly looked at him questioningly. Did Mark really mean that? But he was still grinning. What a neat guy!

"Bye!" she called out. Mark turned and ran across the street. Molly hoped he wasn't just being polite and that he really did want to be her friend.

When she got home she saw a yellow note with her name on it stuck on the front door: *Billy and I have gone to buy some things he must have for school tomorrow. Be back soon. Love, Mom.*

Molly told herself she was too old to expect her mother to be at home for her after her first day in a new school. Hadn't Mom taken her there this morning? She dropped her heavy load of books on the stone steps and got out her new door key.

She examined the keyhole in the doorknob and her shiny new house key and tried to remember how her mom had said to do it. Upside down or right side up? Turn to the left or to the right? She tried them all. The door wouldn't open. She wasn't good at keys. She'd hardly ever used one. In Spring Grove they locked a door only when they went away on vacation.

She stared at the glistening brass doorknob until it became blurry from tears that insisted on coming. A wave of anger washed over her as she thought of her mother leaving her alone to try to get into this empty house. She grabbed the knob with one hand and turned the key with the other. Like magic, the door opened.

She gathered up her books and hurried inside, closing the door. Blitzen was there to greet her, jumping up and barking for attention.

"Hello, boy. Kind of quiet in this big house, isn't it?" She tickled his favorite spot behind his ears. He followed her to the hall closet, continuing to bark happily while she hung up her coat.

A nagging thought told her that she should be doing something important right away. What was it? She shrugged and walked to the kitchen and opened the refrigerator. She was starving.

She reached for the last container of blueberry yogurt when she suddenly heard a high pitched squeal that turned into a long wail.

The burglar alarm!

She ran to the front hall and stared at the confusing panel of buttons and numbers. What were those code numbers? While she tried to remember, the alarm shrieked louder.

Blitzen sat on his haunches, threw back his sleek head and began to howl along with the alarm. He sounded like a wolf answering the call of the wild. Molly stuck her fingers in her ears and closed her eyes. The noise vibrated all through her.

# Five

WITH the burglar alarm shrieking and Blitzen howling, Molly tried to stay calm and remember what her dad said. May 23, her parents' anniversary!

May—May was the fifth month. She punched the number five button, then two and three.

The terrible noise stopped, and Blitzen stopped his howling. How good the silence felt! Relieved, Molly patted the big dog on the back.

"Sorry the noise hurt your ears, Blitzen. We're both learning about life in the big city."

The Weimaraner looked at her with his golden eyes. He probably misses Spring Grove more than any of us, she thought. There he had been free to wander all over town. Everyone knew Blitzen. Here there was a leash law. No dog could go outside the yard without being on a leash.

"Poor Blitzen."

She rubbed his ears, and Blitzen put his big paw on her arm, blissfully happy that someone was talking to him.

"I wish I had a friend to talk with too, ol' boy." In Spring Grove she might have telephoned Brooke after school. Here she didn't know anyone she could call.

A sudden bang-bang-bang on the front door startled her. Blitzen growled, and Molly put him in the kitchen. Then she looked out the front window to see who was there before she unfastened the two locks and opened the door.

"D.C. Police, miss. Is this the Spalding residence?"

A uniformed officer with a gun in his belt stood there, and she could see another policeman waiting at the curb in a police car. Molly shivered.

"Yes," she said weakly. "What's wrong, sir?"

"We got a signal that your burglar alarm had gone off."

What have I done? Molly thought. If Mr.

Lawson finds out about this, he'll make fun of us in his column. Another headline flashed across her mind: "POLICE VISIT CONGRESSMAN SPALDING'S HOUSE."

She tried to smile, but her mouth wouldn't open right.

"I'm sorry," she stammered. "I'm Molly Spalding, and I forgot to turn off the burglar alarm when I got home. It was my first day of school and. . . . You won't tell the newspapers, will you?" She finished lamely.

The officer grinned. "Don't you worry, miss. This happens all the time, especially with new residents. I bet you didn't have a burglar alarm where you came from."

"No, sir. Not in Spring Grove, Texas. We— we didn't even lock the doors there."

"Hey, I'm a Texan, too. I hail from out Amarillo way. Name's Randolph Knott, and I'm on duty in your neighborhood. So if there's anything I can help you with, you just let me know. Bye now, Molly."

Molly closed the door, turned the locks, and reset the alarm. She felt better. Getting used to a new town was harder than she expected, but there were friendly people in Washington.

* * * * *

After Meeting the next morning, Mrs. Gale came over to Molly and said, "The Headmaster would like to see you now."

Molly left the room as quietly as possible, but she felt that everyone was looking at her. Why would the Headmaster want to see her after only one day? Maybe Shipton didn't want her here after all.

Mr. Chipman greeted her pleasantly and asked her to sit down. Then he got right to the point.

"Molly, your teachers have told me they are covering some material in seventh grade math and language arts that you haven't had yet." His voice was quiet but firm.

He's probably going to tell me I'll have to leave, Molly thought. She made her hands into fists and held her breath so she wouldn't cry. She had failed already.

"I will tell your parents about this," he went on, "but I want to talk to you first. You can do one of two things. You can move into the sixth grade here. It's about the level of your school in Spring Grove. Or . . . "

"No! No! Not sixth grade again," Molly

exclaimed, surprising both of them with her outburst.

"—or you can be tutored at noon and after school in math and language arts to catch up to your class grade," Mr. Chipman finished smoothly.

"Yes, yes, that's what I want. A tutor," Molly said, vigorously nodding her head. The palms of her hands were wet and clammy. What would her friends in Spring Grove think if she had to repeat a grade?

Mr. Chipman smiled. "You seem to know what you want to do, Molly. Do you understand that by choosing tutoring you won't have much time to socialize and make friends in the next few months? You won't be in the lunchroom at noon, and you won't be able to go out for after school sports such as lacrosse or tennis. You'll be with the tutor during those times."

"But I will stay in the seventh grade that way, right?" Mr. Chipman had to know she meant to do her best.

The headmaster got up and reached out to shake hands. "It's a deal, Molly. If you work hard, you should be able to catch up with your class by the end of the semester, or maybe sooner. I'll call your parents to let them know what you decided. If it's okay with them, you can start tomorrow."

The next day at lunch time Molly found her way to a room with the sign on the door that said "TUTORING." She knocked, and the door was opened quickly by a small, middle-aged woman with black and silver hair cut trimly and who wore an attractive print dress. She greeted Molly with a smile.

"I'll bet you're Molly," she said. "I'm Mrs. Miller, and I'll help you get up to speed in math and language arts."

Lunch for two was already set on a small table, and they became acquainted as they ate. Mrs. Miller had a calm, easy voice, and she had a way of explaining things that made them seem perfectly clear. She was very sure of herself, and somehow she made Molly feel the same way.

Algebra wasn't easy. Molly still felt as if she were trying to learn a foreign language. After a half hour, Mrs. Miller switched to English grammar and began to explain how to diagram sentences.

When the bell rang at the end of the period Mrs. Miller said, "I'll see you after school, Molly. I guess you realize you're not going to have much free time for the next few months."

"I know, but do you think they'll put me back in the sixth grade?" That was the big question.

"It's up to you, Molly, and how hard you work. The work won't be easy, but it's not impossible. See you after school."

As the days passed, Molly found that Mrs. Miller and the Headmaster were right. Catching up at this school was a full-time job. She hardly knew the names of the other seventh graders because she didn't have time to talk to them. Ashley, the girl across the aisle from Molly in homeroom, seemed friendly. She showed Molly what book to get out for each subject.

Jocelyn, the senator's daughter who was supposed to live a few blocks from her, sat on the far side of the room. Somehow Molly never got to talk to her because Jocelyn was always surrounded by a circle of friends. Molly hoped that some day she might run into her on the subway.

When Mark stayed late for sports and Molly for tutoring, they often met going to the subway. She liked that. Mark knew so much about the city, about Congress, and about school that she always learned something new when she rode with him. Besides, he was fun. She liked him a lot.

After two weeks, Molly felt she was really making progress. One Saturday morning she woke up with the wonderful feeling that she could stay in bed late. She didn't have to bundle up and run out in the cold to the subway. She snuggled down under the covers.

She thought about inviting someone to come over the way she used to in Spring Grove on Saturdays. But she remembered that she didn't know anyone well enough to call on the phone—unless she called someone in Texas.

A lonely, empty feeling crept over her. Molly got up quickly to shake the feeling.

She would write to Brooke. After that she could tackle that mountain of homework on her desk, including the report that was due on Monday. She knew she really didn't have time for friends, just as Mr. Chipman had warned her. Billy, on the other hand, had the house full of his friends every day when she got home from school.

It's more important to stay in the seventh grade than to have friends, she told herself. In the eighth grade I'll have plenty of time to make friends.

She reached into her desk for the letter that came from Brooke yesterday. She read it again. Brooke had enclosed a clipping from the *Spring Grove Sentinel*. A photo showed the four Spaldings entering the Capitol for the swearing-in ceremony.

"You had the biggest smile of all on your face," Brooke wrote in her round handwriting on the pink flowered stationery. "You must be the happiest one in the family to be in Washington."

Should she tell Brooke about her lion-tamer smile, and that she had pretended the photographers were lions? Better not put it in writing, she decided.

A delicious smell floated up from downstairs. Dad was making pancakes! Back in Spring Grove he made pancakes every Saturday morning. She hurried into her jeans. Homework could wait.

Dad was so busy being a new congressman that she had hardly seen him since school started. He didn't get home until long after she and Billy had dinner at night, and she was usually deep into her homework when he came in. Some nights he and Mom had to go to dinner parties, he in a tuxedo he called his "monkey suit," and Mom in one of her new long dresses with spangles and rhinestones.

"Morning, darling," her dad greeted her. "Where's the rest of the family?"

She ran to the stairs and called, "Mom! Billy! Saturday pancakes!"

The telephone rang as she came back into the kitchen.

"Tell him I'm not available, Molly," Dad called out from the stove.

Molly picked up the phone. "Spalding residence."

"Good morning. This is Jack Stratton from Eagle Bend. May I speak with Congressman Spalding, please?"

"I'm sorry but he's not available right now."

Molly looked over at her father. He was nodding his head encouragingly.

"Will you please leave your number, and I'll ask him to call you back."

At the stove, Dad smiled and waved to

Molly with the pancake turner.

"Thank you very much for your message and phone number, Mr. Stratton." She hung up.

"Very good, Molly. Very professional. That Mr. Stratton has an appointment with me early Monday morning. He doesn't need to talk to me now."

"Dad, I feel like I'm telling a lie when you're right here."

"I'm here physically," Dad answered, "but I'm not available to a caller at 8:30 on Saturday morning. No congressman should be expected to work 24 hours a day. Saturday morning is for you and Billy and your mom. You're protecting our privacy."

"I agree," Mom said, coming in and sitting down at the table. "Protecting privacy is something a congressman's family has to do to survive in Washington. Even so, your father and I have to go out to lunch today with a few folks from Texas and to dinner tonight with some senators. So let's enjoy a quiet breakfast."

"Hey, isn't anyone going to eat my delicious pancakes?" Dad asked.

Billy had just come in, and he put his

plate out for Dad to fill. Mom found the maple syrup and served the sausages.

It's our Saturday morning tradition moved to Washington, Molly thought, but it's taken us three Saturdays to get to it. And it's been more than a week since we all had a meal together.

Soon they were talking and laughing just like old times. Molly felt the warmth as she looked contentedly at her mom and dad, and at Billy drowning his pancakes in syrup. When will we all be together again? she wondered.

"I'm in the Daredevils reading group, Dad," Billy said. "In a couple of months Miss Wilson thinks I might be a Champion, when I can read in the book they're reading. We had different books with different words in Spring Grove."

"I thought we were all reading English," Molly said in a low voice.

"But they're not the same words," Billy answered angrily. "I'll show you my vocabulary list."

Mom gave Molly a look that said, "Stop picking on your little brother." Molly felt a little guilty then, especially when she saw that Billy was near tears. Moving was hard on him too, she realized, even with all his new friends. Then she remembered a complaint she had been saving up to tell her dad.

"You didn't warn me how hard Shipton Friends was going to be," she said. "It's a lot different from Spring Grove. As you know, my tutor is teaching me algebra, and I'm learning how to diagram sentences in language arts with her, too."

"I know it must be tough for you," he answered. "You're a lot like me. You always do best when faced with a challenge. I know Shipton's a tough school. But I've heard that Mrs. Miller is an outstanding tutor. You can survive there. Your mom and I will help you all we can."

The phone rang again and Molly reached to answer it. "Are you here yet, Dad?"

"Gone 'til Monday."

"Spalding residence, Molly speaking."

"Good morning, Molly," said a smooth, friendly voice. "This is Clayton Lawson."

"Oh, good morning, Mr. Lawson," Molly said, saying the man's name slowly to get her father's attention. She looked at her dad questioningly. He nodded, threw down his breakfast fork angrily, and reached for the phone.

"Claytie, what's on your mind this early?" he said breezily. He might have been greeting a very good friend,

Molly thought, Dad's a good actor.

"I see," the congressman said after listening for a little while. "No, I'm not about to take a trip to Barbados with the Banking Committee." He laughed a little weakly. "I just got on the committee, Claytie. Besides, I don't know what banking business we would have with Barbados. You know that I campaigned against that kind of junketing around by members of Congress. It'll be a long time before I take a government paid trip anywhere, except back to Texas to report to my constituents."

Molly heard Dad say good-bye and hung up. He looked annoyed for a few seconds. Then he laughed. "Old Claytie thought he had me going off on a free trip to the Caribbean with my new committee. Wouldn't that make a good headline in the Texas newspapers? 'NOVICE CONGRESSMAN SPALDING FLIES OFF ON JUNKET TO BARBADOS.'"

"Maybe I should have said you weren't here, Dad," Molly said.

"No," he replied, reaching for another pancake. "I'll always talk to Claytie. I have to. If you had said I wasn't here, he would have assumed I was avoiding him because I was planning to join the committee on the free trip. Who knows what he would have implied in his column? We have to keep in touch with reporters, no matter what. Even though reporters irritate me sometimes, I know they help keep our nation healthy by keeping watch over the political process, which includes people like me."

Looking out the window, Molly could see a bit of the Capitol dome from the breakfast nook. She remembered how thrilled and excited she had been to see it her first night in Washington. But there was a price to pay for living in Washington—little time for the family and always a fight for privacy.

# Six

"I don't like to leave you alone on Sunday," Molly's mom said apologetically. She stood in the front hall in her new plaid suit, saying good-bye to Molly and Billy as she waited for her husband to come downstairs. "I wouldn't go, except that the Speaker of the House invited us to brunch. He's Dad's boss—in a way."

"Tell the Speaker he should have invited Billy and me," Molly snapped. She was short on understanding this morning.

"I wouldn't go even if I were invited," Billy said flatly. "They'll probably have caviar and those smelly dips. Ugh!" He made a terrible face.

The congressman called out to Molly and

Billy as he rounded a turn of the staircase. "Kids, please take Blitzen out for a walk. He wanders around this house like a prisoner."

"He is one, Dad, because of that leash law. He used to mosey all over Spring Grove." Billy patted the big dog and rubbed his ears. "Wanna go for a walk?"

At the magic word "walk" Blitzen barked his enthusiastic "Yes!" Then he sat like a stone statue while Billy attached the leash to his collar. "We won't be too late; I'm really sorry about this," their mother said as the couple hurried off.

"Molly, let's go buy half-smokes for lunch," Billy suggested.

"What's that?"

"Fatter than a hot dog and tastes a lot better. They sell them at a stand outside the Air and Space Museum. My friend Scott and I had them yesterday when his mother took us to see the astronaut exhibits."

"Okay, Billy. Mom gave me lunch money, and I'll try anything once." She went to the closet. "Let's wear those new down jackets Mom bought us. It's pretty cold this morning." She tossed Billy's red jacket to him before putting on her blue one. "Now, don't open the door until we're all ready. Blitzen goes crazy when he sees the outdoors."

When they were both ready, Molly turned on the burglar alarm by punching in the code. Then she opened the door and held on to the leash as tightly as she could. Blitzen pulled Molly down the front steps, straining at the leash while she and Billy yelled at him to stop.

"He'd better learn to walk on this leash, or Dad says he'll have to go to an obedience school." Molly looked threateningly at the Weimaraner. His golden eyes stared back trustingly. As if Blitzen understood, he let Molly lead him down Independence Avenue's sidewalk. He walked properly beside her, as if he were on display in a dog show.

A squirrel suddenly darted across the sidewalk. Blitzen leaped forward, forgetting the leash.

"Heel, Blitzen, heel!" Molly shouted. She grabbed the leash with both hands. The powerful dog bounded after the squirrel and pulled Molly down the sidewalk. The squirrel scooted to safety up a tree. Blitzen stood under it, barking determinedly at the treed squirrel as any good hunting dog should.

A few blocks and two squirrels later, they reached the Air and Space Museum.

Billy pointed to the curb, where vans were parked along the entire length of the block. "Scott's Mom said that min-or-i-ties get licenses to sell things from these vans." He said "minorities" very carefully, as if he had learned the word yesterday. "A Vietnamese family sells the half-smokes I want."

Billy led the way, checking out each vehicle. In each van, vendors were selling T-shirts, postcards, candy bars, hot dogs— almost anything a tourist might want. Except half-smokes.

"They must be here somewhere," Billy insisted, leading Molly and Blitzen past the museum.

"Will you settle for a hot dog?" Molly asked. Even with her hooded jacket, she was getting cold.

"No!" Billy almost shouted. "Half-smokes are much better."

He walked ahead stubbornly, and in the next block he found the right van. He pointed triumphantly to the sign on a big silver van: "HALF-SMOKES, $1.50."

Molly handed the leash to Billy while she went to the sliding glass window at the side of the van to buy their lunch. An Asian girl, about Molly's age, opened the window. She was wearing a warm-looking ski jacket with a white, fur-trimmed hood.

"Two half-smokes, please," Molly said. She couldn't help adding, "I've never even seen a half-smoke. We didn't eat them where we used to live."

The Asian girl looked up as she wrapped a hot dog bun around a fat sausage. It seemed to Molly as if the girl wanted to know more.

"I—I come from Texas," Molly stammered. "Do you know where that is?"

The girl nodded and grinned broadly. Molly wondered if she could understand her.

"We don't eat them where I used to live either," the girl said in perfect English. "I come from Vietnam."

The girls laughed together. A friend is someone you can laugh with, Molly thought. And here's someone my own age who knows how scary and lonely it is to move to a new place. She even had to learn to speak a new language, and she did it just fine. That's much harder than learning algebra and grammar and what a half-smoke is.

Molly passed the catsup bottle to Billy and put mustard on her sausage.

"My name is Molly," she said. "I live up on that hill." With mustard on her finger she indicated the area near the Capitol.

"I'm Kwai—K-W-A-I." I live across the river in Arlington." She pointed in the opposite direction.

Other customers came to the van, and Molly and Billy moved out of the way. When the people left, Molly went up to the window again.

Molly held her breath and took a chance.

"Uh, I know this is sort of crazy, but if I come back next Saturday, would you like to do something together?"

Kwai nodded and smiled. "When my mother and father are both here, I can leave the van. We could go into the Air and Space Museum or any of the other Smithsonian buildings. I know them all. I spent almost every day last summer in them while my parents worked here."

A quick smile lit up her face. "Only don't

bring the dog. They don't let dogs into the museums."

Kwai raised her hand in a good-bye wave, then leaned forward to her next customer.

Eating their half-smokes, Molly and Billy walked back toward Capitol Hill.

"You're right, Billy," Molly agreed. "A half-smoke tastes much better than a plain old hot dog. And I liked that girl Kwai who sells them. Thanks, brother." She gave him a pat on the shoulder.

As they hiked back up the avenue, Billy held the leash, and the powerful gray dog practically pulled him up the incline. Running behind them, Molly felt something damp on her face.

"Oh, Billy, it's starting to rain."

But it wasn't rain. She looked more closely and saw that the sky was full of little white specks. "Billy, Billy, it's snowing!" Molly shrieked with excitement. "Look!" She held out her arm, now nearly covered with the white specks.

"It's snow! Real snow!" Billy shouted.

Over the next several minutes the snow began to change the world around them. It wasn't like the noisy rain that splattered on you during a Texas downpour, Molly thought. This was a silent kind of magic.

The snow came down fast and heavy. A white carpet began to cover the grass and stick to the trees along Independence Avenue.

Snow gathered on top of Blitzen's flat head, and an occasional flake hit Molly right in the eye.

She put out a gloved hand to catch snowflakes. "Billy, I wonder if it's true like it says in our science books that each snowflake has a different design."

"Snow! Snow! Snow!" Billy shouted, running up and down the sidewalk.

This is great. I've always wanted to see snow, Molly thought. It's even better than I imagined. With everything turning white, it's almost like being in an ice palace.

In a short time everything around her looked different. The brick townhouses of Capitol Hill were dusted with a white frosting, and a quiet kind of peace filled the air as the snow continued to fall.

A station wagon passed, its wheels spinning as it skidded on the snow-covered street.

"It's Mom and Dad," Billy said. Dad turned the car into the driveway, and it skidded on the incline to the garage.

"It's snowing! It's snowing!" Billy yelled, as if he were the only one who could see it.

Dad got out, stooped down, and disappeared behind the car. He came back up with something in his hands.

"You mean this is snow?" he asked. He threw a snowball, first hitting Billy in the chest. Then he made another and threw it at Molly, hitting her on the shoulder. In a few seconds Molly made her first snowball and hit him back.

Molly's mom got out of the car and was pelted by all of them before she could make her first snowball. What fun snow is, Molly thought. I hope it keeps snowing until it's five feet deep.

\* \* \* \* \*

In the morning, snow covered nearly everything. From her tower room windows, Molly couldn't even see where the streets should be. Huge white mounds showed where two cars had parked. No cars were moving on Capitol Hill, and it was still snowing.

Mrs. Spalding was listening to the radio in the kitchen. "I'm trying to hear if your schools have been closed."

At the half hour, the news announcer started with a long list of school closings for the day. He named schools starting with A, then B, and then he said, "Capitol Hill Day School—closed."

"Hooray!" Billy called. "No school for me!"

It seemed to take the announcer forever to reach S. Maybe Shipton would stay open, Molly thought. Maybe those plain Quakers thought it was a good test of character to struggle through snow to school. She'd probably have to walk through those snowdrifts to the subway while Billy stayed home and had all the fun.

"Shipton Friends School—closed today," the announcer said at last.

"Hooray for Shipton!" Molly cheered. Those Quakers weren't so bad after all.

"You may be cheering, but I know the House of Representatives will be in session, no matter what," her dad said.

He went to the garage and came back

with a brand new shovel. "Good thing I bought this as soon as I got here," he said.

He started out the door with his pant legs stuffed into an old pair of cowboy boots and a plaid muffler tied around neck, feeling where the steps might be under the deep snow. He shoveled off the steps and made a trail out to the front gate. Then he shoveled off the driveway before he left for work.

"Mom, we're going out to play in the snow," Billy yelled as he zipped up his down jacket.

"Let's make a snowman, Molly," Billy said when got outside.

Molly looked around the drifted snow in the yard. There certainly was enough snow here for dozens of snowmen. But how do you do it? she wondered.

She tried to make a snowball, but this morning it didn't work. Billy tried, too, but the cold, powdery snow couldn't be gathered into anything like a ball.

In books kids always make a snowman as soon as there's a snowstorm, Molly thought. What's wrong with this Washington snow? She hated to admit failure to Billy. He was so excited.

As Molly looked up, she saw two boys

standing at the front gate. Their quilted jackets with hoods and mufflers almost covered their faces.

"Hi," said one of the boys.

Molly looked more closely at the taller one and recognized Mark. He and his little brother Freddie were pulling sleds and carrying a big, round plastic thing that looked like a garbage can lid.

"Where are you going?" Billy asked. "Are you going to ride on those sleds?"

"Yeah," Freddie answered. "What are you doing?"

"We were going to make a snowman," Billy said.

"Can't make a snowman this morning," Mark asserted. "It's too cold. The temperature dropped drastically in the middle of the night. Now it's too cold for the snow to stick together. You'd better wait 'til it warms up, and the snow begins to melt a little. Probably tomorrow."

Billy looked crushed, and Molly felt sorry for him. "I can't make a snowman now? What can I do then? We don't have any sleds. This is the first time we've ever seen snow."

"Come with us, Billy," Freddie said.

"Go ask your mom first," Mark added. While the two little boys were inside, Mark said, "Put those two together, and they could end up anywhere, even Hawaii. Uh, Molly, do you want to go with us, too? All the kids go sledding down Capitol Hill. It's a neat place, and the Capitol Police don't mind if we have some fun."

"Thanks, Mark." Molly tried to be cool and not to sound too excited, but she was thrilled that he had included her.

They took off for the Capitol grounds making a new trail in the blanket of snow covering the ground. A group of kids had gathered there already and were making crisscross patterns across the face of the hill with their sleds.

Molly soon found out that the plastic things were called saucers. "You can't really steer a saucer," Mark said, as he pointed out a downhill trail for her. You just hold on to the sides and hope for the best."

Molly got into the saucer and Mark gave her a solid push on her shoulders. Off she went. The ride was fast and fun, and she ended up in a snowbank. Molly could hardly wait to get back up the hill to try again.

Next she tried sitting on a sled for the ride to the bottom and then graduated to lying on her stomach on a sled and steering it. After that, Mark talked her into trying the steeper, longer runs. Billy was also learning how to steer a sled with some help from his new friend Freddie.

"Hey, here are two other Shipton kids," Mark said. "It's the Scott twins, Towanda and Bennett. They're in the eighth grade."

He greeted sister and brother, and introduced Molly and Billy.

"Haven't I seen you around Shipton?" Towanda asked Molly.

"I'm a new student. Started in 7C second semester," Molly said.

"It's hard at first in a new school," Towanda said. "Meeting all those strange people. We hardly get any new kids at midyear, so it's easy for me to recognize you."

As a place opened at the steepest hill, Towanda put her sled down. She smiled at Molly, "Want to take this hill on my sled?"

Of course Molly would, and Towanda got her going with a good solid push. Molly seemed to be going as fast as the wind, and she forgot to steer. She ended up rolling off into the snow. It felt great. She lay in the snow for a few seconds, just enjoying it. Then she got up, eager to go back up to the top of the hill.

As the morning went on, more neighborhood kids with sleds and saucers came. They sledded all morning, dashed home for a quick lunch, and headed back to Capitol Hill again.

Jocelyn arrived in the middle of the afternoon, pulling a long, wooden toboggan. "Hi, sure am glad I found you Shipton guys. I thought I might have to go down on this monster sled all alone. Come on, let's pile on."

"All of us?" Molly asked. She wondered where seven people were going to fit.

"Biggest ones on the bottom, medium-sized in their laps, and the little kids on top," she said.

Jocelyn made everything seem like fun. They moved to the steepest hill of all, and piled on the toboggan in layers. Mark and Towanda and Bennett sat down first, then Jocelyn and Molly in their laps, and Freddie and Billy on top of them.

They pushed off with a "Whoop!" when

another kid on the hilltop gave them a shove. Down the hill they went, screaming all the way. The toboggan ended up in a snowbank next to Independence Avenue with everyone laughing. By the third time they'd done it, Molly couldn't remember anything ever being more fun.

The tobogganers stayed until the street lights came on, and the day faded into dusk. Then they all started off for home in one boisterous bunch with some kids leaving the group as they reached the different parts of Capitol Hill close to where they lived.

Molly walked alongside Jocelyn for several blocks. This was the first time Molly had a chance to talk with her. In school Jocelyn always seemed to be surrounded by a group of friends, and there was no way for a newcomer to break in.

Trying to think of something they both had in common, Molly asked, "How's your country report for Mr. Wolff going?"

"I have Scotland," Jocelyn said. "We were only there four days, so I didn't have time to get much stuff! My Mom bought me a tam o'shanter—that's a kind of Scottish hat." She laughed. "I guess I can wear that on my head while I give my report."

Jocelyn turned away, pulling her toboggan behind her. "I go off here on South Carolina Avenue," she said. "See you guys in school tomorrow. Good-bye, gang."

When Molly and Billy got home, they made hot chocolate. Molly couldn't remember a more wonderful day. To think she had gone twelve long years of her life without snow.

By eight o'clock she had finished dinner, taken a hot bath and gone upstairs to the tower room to write to her friend in Texas.

"Dear Brooke," she began. "Today our school, and nearly everything else in Washington, was closed because of a snowstorm. We went sledding and tobogganing down Capitol Hill instead. What fun . . ."

# Seven

MOLLY woke up to sunshine and realized with relief that at long last Saturday had come again. No school, no tutoring, and Dad's day to make pancakes for breakfast. She got into her robe and slippers and started downstairs. When she reached the hall, she saw her dad at the closet putting on his new, black cashmere overcoat.

He reached out and gave her a hug. The coat felt soft and velvety against Molly's cheeks as she returned the hug.

"Sorry, Molly, but I have to run off to a breakfast at the Capitol. No pancakes today. See you later, darling."

He grinned—the great grin that was on a

thousand campaign posters she had helped tack up last fall. For a moment she felt her familiar pride—her dad, now a famous congressman.

He tapped the burglar alarm buttons quickly and started to open the door. Then, he stopped. Remembering the rolled-up newspaper in his pocket, he turned back and gave it to Molly.

"I forgot about this. There's an item about me in Claytie's column in the *Spring Grove Sentinel.* Show it to Mom, will you?"

He waved good-bye and closed the door.

Molly felt her pride turn to anger and disappointment. How could he skip breakfast again this morning? They hadn't had one meal together since last Saturday. Dad left for the office now every morning before she woke up, and he and Mom went off to meetings or formal dinners several nights each week. Suddenly she hated that big white Capitol. It had swallowed her Dad into its dome.

With a pang of loneliness, Molly looked at the newspaper, which had been folded open to the editorial page. Mom walked down the stairs and read the article with her. Marked in red was Clayton Lawson's "Report from Capitol Hill."

## NO BARBADOS TRIP YET, OUR JUSTIN SAYS

Many of the House Banking Committee members have taken off on an Air Force plane to the Island of Barbados, supposedly on an inspection tour of that island. Rumor has it that they, and their wives, are chiefly inspecting the beaches of this lush tropical island.

Our freshman congressman, Justin Spalding, newly appointed to that committee, was very much at home when we phoned him about this trip last Saturday morning. He said that he had no intention of going on any junkets at taxpayers' expense.

Keep tuned, however. Maybe on some cold, wintery day in Washington in the future, the Spaldings will feel a sudden urge to inspect a nice warm place, such as Barbados, Tahiti, or Hawaii, with the committee.

"Typical Lawson writing," Mrs. Spalding said, shaking her head. "A little bit of truth and a lot that's not."

"How can he write something like that, Mom?" Molly was enraged. "When Mr. Lawson called, you heard Dad say that he would never take a free trip. Can't Dad write the newspaper and demand a correction? Or sue or something? It's not fair."

"No, it's not, Molly," her mom agreed. "But it's such a little thing, we'll smile and overlook it. Something more important might come up that Dad will insist the paper correct. Remember, the *Sentinel* didn't support Dad for Congress."

Billy rushed downstairs and called out to Molly. "Am I late? Jason's birthday party is at 11:45, and my clock isn't working."

"You've got plenty of time, Billy," Molly answered. "We haven't even had breakfast, yet."

Later, while Billy struggled with his jacket zipper, Molly went to the mantel and picked up the birthday present she had wrapped for him to take.

"Thanks, Molly. It looks great," he called out as he ran out the door and down the block to his friend's house. Molly remembered that she hadn't been to a birthday party since they had moved to Washington. Billy was invited to one nearly every week.

She found herself hoping the telephone would ring. In Spring Grove on Saturdays she got so many calls that it used to be a family joke. "Molly's phone is ringing again!"

Dad would tease. It certainly wasn't ringing now, and it wasn't going to. No one knew her well enough to call, except Mrs. Miller or Mrs. Gale. All she had time for now at school was going for tutoring so she could catch up.

Suddenly she thought of one person she did know: Kwai, the girl at the half-smokes van in front of the Air and Space Museum. She remembered Kwai's nice smile and all the changes in Kwai's life. Molly decided to walk over to the museum. She had a school assignment she could work on there this morning, and she could look for Kwai too.

Molly walked down Independence Avenue to the museum and saw the silver van parked at the curb. She went up to the glass window, and Kwai's father slid it open.

"Good morning. I came to see Kwai," Molly said.

"Here I am," said Kwai, appearing from the other end of the van. She looked different this morning. She was wearing a long blue silk dress over white satin pants. On her head she wore a simple gold crown.

"Kwai, Remember me? We talked a couple of weeks ago when my brother and I bought half-smokes."

"Oh, yes, I remember," Kwai said. You didn't bring your brother today."

"No, he's at a skating party," Molly said. She brightened. "You said you'd show me a museum if I didn't bring Blitzen. And look—no dog!"

Molly held up her empty hands. Both girls laughed.

"Maybe this isn't a good time," Molly said, making it easy for Kwai to say no. "You're all dressed up."

"Today is Tet, the Vietnamese New Year," Kwai explained. "It's the most important Vietnamese holiday, so I wore this dress today. It's like what a Vietnamese bride wears to her wedding." She turned around proudly in the small space in the van.

"It's very pretty, Kwai."

"Let me ask my father if I can leave," Kwai said. She turned around and spoke to her father in Vietnamese. After a quick discussion, Kwai came out of the van, and the two girls hurried into the museum.

"My friend Mark said there's an exhibit with five or six pioneer woman aviators, and Amelia Earhart is one of them. I have to do a report on her."

Kwai's eyes lit up. "I know exactly where it is," she said eagerly.

Kwai turned on her heel and marched directly across the museum, under the Wright Brothers' first airplane, then past Charles Lindbergh's "Spirit of Saint Louis."

"Go left now, this is faster," Kwai said, half over her shoulder, leading Molly along a side way that avoided the crowds. Kwai knew the museum as well as a guide. They walked up a little-used staircase beyond the escalators. In a minute they were standing at the exhibit of women in aviation.

"Amelia Earhart, Molly," Kwai said. She pointed to a life-size figure of the woman aviator dressed in a flight suit. Molly read the exhibit labels and took notes.

"Kwai, look, it says Amelia Earhart was wearing an outfit like this when she disappeared over the Pacific Ocean." Molly looked at Kwai. "I guess it wasn't too awfully far from Vietnam where she went down. At least, a lot closer to Vietnam than to Washington."

"Vietnam is on the Pacific Ocean," Kwai explained. She shook her head slowly. "But it's a very, very big ocean."

A sad, faraway look passed over Kwai's face—a look Molly had not seen before. "Yes, that ocean was terribly big and very frightening. We were what they call 'boat people,' you know. We escaped from Vietnam on a small boat and waited in a refugee camp for two awful years before we could come here." She paused. "My little brother got sick and died in that camp. When I think of the Pacific Ocean, I think of him."

"I'm sorry, Kwai."

Kwai brushed away some tears quickly. "Soon after that we got our papers and flew to the United States. We've been here four years."

"And you speak English perfectly, Kwai," Molly couldn't help saying.

Kwai took a quick look at her wrist-watch.

"I have to go help my father sell half-smokes, Molly. It's nearly lunchtime, and my mother's at home getting ready for our Tet celebration tonight. Next time you come to see me, I'll have more time."

"I can come next Saturday unless my father stays home, but he hardly ever does anymore," Molly said as they hurried out of the museum. "Happy New Year, Kwai!"

Molly waved as her new friend disappeared into her family's van. As she walked home, Molly thought about Kwai. Only six years ago she had left Vietnam in a boat and had survived terrible things—even losing her brother. And still she had kept her a sense of humor and was so good-natured.

I should be able to adjust to a big city and a busy father and a hard school, Molly told herself. I didn't have to cross the ocean and go to a school without knowing any English. She walked a little faster to get up to the top of Capitol Hill.

Maybe the first few months here are the hardest, Molly thought.

# *Eight*

M R. Wolff began the current events discussion in class on Monday by writing the words "GUN CONTROL" on the board.

"That is a very controversial subject today," he said. We probably have students in this class whose families have strong feelings and opinions on both sides of this issue. Let's have a short debate on Wednesday morning. I'll need one volunteer to speak in favor of gun control and one student to speak out against it. Then each speaker will have time for a two-minute rebuttal."

Molly raised her hand quickly. She didn't know anything about the subject, and she'd only seen a debate once during her father's campaign, but she wanted to get some attention in this class. She'd been so quiet all these weeks that she felt that she had become almost invisible. Participating in a debate would be a way to get herself noticed. Mom and Dad would help her. She raised her hand high and caught Mr. Wolff's eye.

"Okay, Molly, which side do you favor? Are you for or against gun control?" Mr. Wolff asked.

She didn't know enough about the subject to have an opinion. Jocelyn had said that Vivian Keegan's father had lost the election on gun control, but whether he had been for or against it she didn't know.

"For it," she stated, just to say something.

"Now who will debate against it?" Several hands went up this time. Mr. Wolff looked all around the room and pointed to Mark.

Molly looked over at him and caught his eye. He smiled back at her quickly. He was going to be a good speaker, she thought. Maybe too good.

That night as they were finishing dinner, the first time they had eaten together all week, Molly brought up the subject of gun control.

"Gun control," her father echoed. "That's Shipton Friends for you. They make you think about what's going on in the real world. I'll tell you my opinion, Molly, but you'll have to make up your own mind. Texans love their guns. When the governor of Texas ran for office, she even took sharpshooting lessons during the campaign to show she wasn't against guns."

"Are you for or against gun control, Dad?" Molly asked.

"I'm sure you've learned by now at Shipton Friends that Quakers are pacifists and are against any kind of violence. Maybe because I went to that school, some of that thinking rubbed off on me."

Dad continued. "I favor control by the federal government on some kinds of guns. In many states people can buy a cheap revolver called a 'Saturday Night Special.' Those guns shouldn't be sold so easily. And there are semi-automatic weapons readily available that are like small machine guns, capable of shooting a hundred bullets in a few seconds. Why should anyone be able to buy a gun like that over the counter? Those weapons are being used in drug wars that are a disgrace in this country."

Mom joined the discussion, adding, "Some people have been trying to get a law passed to ban Saturday Night Specials since one was used to kill Senator Robert Kennedy in 1968. Then after President Reagan and his press officer Jim Brady were shot with the same kind of weapon in 1982, people tried get a federal gun control law through Congress. They failed again."

Mrs. Spalding shook her head slowly. "I hate to tell you this, Molly, but you've taken on a tough job coming out for gun control in your debate."

Molly sighed. "And the teacher even gave me my choice of sides for the debate."

As her parents talked, she made notes for the talk she would give on Wednesday. Her mind was spinning as she plotted ways to rebut Mark's position.

On Wednesday morning during social studies, Mr. Wolff introduced the debate. "Today we're going to hear about gun control," he said. "Molly, since you're talking in favor of gun control, you will be the first speaker. Mark will answer what you propose, since he has the negative."

Molly walked up in front of the class, carrying a single card with her notes. Suddenly she wished she had gone to a library to read more about the subject.

Adrien raised his hand suddenly. "Mr. Wolff, may I report this debate for the school newspaper? I'm the class reporter, and I haven't sent in any news this month."

"Molly? Mark? Is it all right with you?" Mr. Wolff asked. Molly nodded impatiently, and Mark agreed.

Molly began, "President John Kennedy, his brother Bobby, and President Ronald Reagan were all shot with guns that the gunmen probably wouldn't have had if a federal gun control law had been in effect."

She had practiced that sentence at home, and the class looked shocked when she said it. But Molly hadn't practiced the whole talk. She had been so busy with other homework that she hadn't studied her notes. She'd even forgotten some of the things that she now saw on the card she was holding. She found herself saying, "My father said this" and "My mother told me this."

"And so," Molly ended lamely, "I think we should agree with the Quakers who founded this school and back the Congress in passing a law controlling guns in all fifty states." She had a sudden inspiration and added, "My father, Congressman Spalding, is in favor of such a law, and so am I."

As she sat down, Molly felt that she had given her Mom's and Dad's opinions. And, she thought, I probably shouldn't have quoted Dad without asking him first if I could. But it's too late now.

Mark stood in front of the class looking very relaxed. When everyone was quiet, he stepped forward. "Guns don't kill people," he said. "People kill people."

He waited a second for the slogan to sink in.

"That's what the National Rifle Association says," he said quietly. "This is a Quaker school, and Quakers don't believe in violence—and that includes violence from guns. Some of you may agree with them. But listen to what I have to say."

Molly looked around the room and saw that everyone was alert. He went on. "Gun control is not the answer to stopping killings in our country. I may be in the minority here, but I'm going to convince you what's wrong with having the federal government control guns.

"In the first place, the Second Amendment in the Bill of Rights guarantees the right of a citizen to bear arms. Actually, then, there is a constitutional right for citizens to own guns." Mark talked on, looking at a stack of cards he held in one hand.

"In closing," he said, "I propose that the federal government stay out of gun control. Let each state make its own gun laws, if any are needed. No two states are alike. Certainly a gun law for my home state of Tennessee shouldn't be the same as one for the District of Columbia where I live."

Mark stopped. He grinned like a Cheshire cat, and Molly could feel the class warming to him. "Hunters out in the hills of Tennessee don't need the federal government telling them what kind of gun to buy to shoot rabbits." He pointed to Molly and added, "My worthy opponent thinks a federal law will solve all our gun problems. I don't."

Opponent? Who was that? Molly realized with a jolt that she was his opponent. She flushed hot with anger when she realized some of the kids were laughing. When Mark sat down, someone started to clap.

"None of that," Mr. Wolff said strongly, stopping the applause with an upraised hand. "Molly, you now have two minutes for a rebuttal."

Molly's cheeks burned. She'd been so busy listening to Mark she hadn't thought of points for a rebuttal. She walked up to the front of the room with nothing to say. There was a long, terrible silence.

She cleared her throat and said, "Mark says that guns don't kill people; people kill people. He may be right about that, but in the places where there are no guns, no one gets shot. If we got the guns off the street, there wouldn't be four hundred murders a year in this city. And that's a fact." Almost in a whisper Molly added weakly, "Thank you," and went back to her seat.

Mark got up for his rebuttal, looking completely self-confident. "My opponent has not answered my argument about our Constitutional right to bear arms."

He talked pleasantly, pointing out all the other arguments Molly hadn't answered.

Molly could see that Mark was much better prepared than she was. Just because her parents were lawyers, she shouldn't have counted only on what they said as her arguments. Even so, Mark shouldn't have made her look like a fool.

"Thank you, Molly and Mark," Mr. Wolff said. He moved ahead quickly. "Now, since it's Wednesday, it's time for Caitlin O'Malley to give her report on Ireland."

The red-haired girl looked as if she had come straight to Shipton Friends from Ireland. She wore a fisherman's sweater she had bought in the Aran Islands off Ireland's west coast. She gave her talk and finished by showing slides of her family's trip to the part of Tipperary where her grandparents had been born.

Later, Mr. Wolff came to Molly's desk. "You haven't given me the name of the country you're going to report on in March. Did you check the list to see which countries aren't taken yet?"

Molly nodded vaguely. "Yes, sir. I haven't traveled anywhere except Mexico, and that's been taken already. How about—how about Belgium?"

"Belgium?" Mr. Wolff sounded mystified, but he wrote it down in his book. "Very well, Molly. You will give a fifteen minute presentation on Belgium on March 29th."

The class was finally over, and Molly was getting up to go to lunch when Mark stopped by her desk.

"Molly?" he asked quietly.

She looked away from him, turned her back, and with her chin held high walked out of the room. She would never speak to Mark again. Not ever. He had called her an "opponent." She would stay his "opponent" for life.

What a terrible day, Molly thought as, at last, she went to her homeroom and gathered up her books for her after-school hour with Mrs. Miller. Ashley, usually the first one out of homeroom, was still sitting at her desk.

"Molly." Ashley seemed to hesitate. "I overheard you talking with Mr. Wolff. How did you happen to pick Belgium for a report?"

"To tell the truth," Molly answered, "last night my father was talking about a congressman who owns a Belgian sheepdog.

When Mr. Wolff asked which country I had chosen, I suddenly thought of that big black dog and Belgium just popped into my head. I've never traveled overseas like these other kids. So why not Belgium? What's your country, Ashley?" Somehow she felt that the other girl wanted her to ask.

"It's Sweden. I can't find much about it in the library, and we're not supposed to use encyclopedias, you know." Ashley looked at Molly intensely. "You could do me a big favor, Molly."

"What's that?" Molly asked.

"You kids whose fathers are in the Congress have a really good deal for research. Your father's staff just calls the Library of Congress, and a researcher puts together lots of information on any subject. All the congressmen's kids do it. Where do you think Mark got all that gun control stuff today? I used to ask Vivian Keegan, but she moved away."

As Molly thought it over, Ashley went on quickly, "Don't bother your Dad. He's too busy, I know. Is there someone else in his office you could call?"

"Okay, Ashley, I—I'll try," Molly said. "See you tomorrow."

When she got home after her hour of tutoring with Mrs. Miller, there was a note on the refrigerator door. Billy and her mother had gone to buy him ice skates. A few minutes later, as Molly was starting upstairs with her homework, the telephone rang.

"Hi, Molly. It's Charlotte Frauenheim in your father's office. May I speak to your mother?"

"She's not here, Charlotte. Can she call you later?"

Right then Molly got an idea. Charlotte was always asking Molly what she could do for her.

"Charlotte, I wonder if you could get some information I need for school about Belgium and Sweden. Facts about those countries and what's been happening there lately. Is that something you could do?"

Charlotte hesitated. Then she said it wouldn't be any trouble at all.

"There's no big hurry, Charlotte. We— Uh—I won't be giving the reports for a month."

"I'll call the Library of Congress Research Service right now," Charlotte promised. "Reports on Belgium and Sweden and what's happening there today. Right?"

Molly felt a little guilty about asking for the information. If only congressmen's kids could use the Congressional Research Service, was that fair? What about everyone else in school? Ashley had said that Mark had gotten his information from the research service. If she'd known to use that, she would have given a better talk. It was taking her so long to learn the ropes in this new school.

Molly sighed, picked up her backpack, and went upstairs to do her algebra.

\* \* \* \* \* \*

On Friday Molly saw her name in the *Middle School Echo* for the first time. Adrien's story on the gun control debate was on the front page, headlined "SEVENTH GRADERS DEBATE GUN CONTROL." It said:

> Mark Hathaway and Molly Spalding, whose fathers are both members of Congress, debated gun control in Mr. Wolff's social studies class this week.
>
> Molly, who says her father favors a federal

law controlling some kinds of guns, spoke in favor of gun control. She talked about the many deaths in our cities and assassinations from "Saturday Night Specials," and about drug dealers using automatic weapons.

Mark spoke out against gun control. He quoted from the Bill of Rights on the right to bear arms and from the National Rifle Association.

For a minute or so, Molly was proud to see her name in print. Now more kids would get to know her. But then a nagging doubt began to eat at her, seeing in print that her dad was in favor of gun control. He had never said so in a speech. Had he told her that just for her information and not as a public statement for the media?

Molly decided not to show the school paper to her mom and dad. Instead, she mailed it off to Brooke in Spring Grove, so her friend could see that this school had a newspaper and that Molly had debated a subject they had never even talked about in her Texas school.

# Nine

ON Saturday, Molly and Kwai entered the Air and Space Museum the minute it opened. Kwai confidently led the way to the escalator, so they were the first two to go into the astronauts' Skylab that was hanging in the air above the first floor.

For a few minutes she and Kwai were astronauts, prancing about the cabin and acting weightless, giggling as they leaped about in the replica of the original Skylab. The girls wiggled some of the instruments as they plotted their journey through space. They even made their way around some aliens who had found their way into the galaxy.

The aliens, two chubby Boy Scouts in

uniform, appeared at the entrance, and the girls' space bubble burst. They hurried past the boys and went off to see one of the movies on the museum's giant screen.

The next Saturday Kwai showed Molly the Museum of Natural History.

"Want to see the Hope Diamond?" Kwai asked, then led the way upstairs to the huge gem collection.

They passed hundreds of minerals and crystals, finally working their way to the far wall. There the rare jewels, some of the world's largest—diamonds, rubies, emeralds, sapphires—sparkled behind glass. Many of the gems were set in necklaces and bracelets.

"Which one would you take home, if you could?" Molly asked Kwai.

"I already have my favorite," Kwai said mysteriously. "But you can have any of the others."

Molly walked down the long row of precious gems. The Hope Diamond was big and sparkly, but somehow it looked too heavy to wear. She hesitated in front of a necklace of sapphires as blue as Texas bluebonnets, but now she knew the gems she liked best.

"That's the one I'll take," she said emphatically. She pointed to a sparkling necklace of huge emeralds surrounded by diamonds. "You can have the Hope Diamond, Kwai, and everything else."

"Oh, no, Molly. That emerald necklace is mine," Kwai said, her hands on her hips in indignation. "I picked it out last summer. You'll have to choose something else."

The two looked up and saw six tourists and both museum guards watching them curiously. The girls giggled and moved away. Molly suddenly felt happy that they both chose the same necklace. Friends often like the same things.

At noon she and Kwai agreed to meet the next Saturday, and Kwai hurried off to the van to help her family.

Molly walked home to her ever-waiting homework. It was so good to have a friend. Dad was in Texas seeing voters, and Billy was at another birthday party, this one a bowling party. He sure was having a good time in Washington.

Her dad came back from Texas on Sunday night while Molly and Billy and their mom were having hamburgers in the kitchen. Molly thought Dad looked tired as he came in and put down his suitcase.

"Hi. I had dinner on the plane, so don't worry about me, Joan," he said. "Charlotte is coming here on a press matter. Molly, please bring her to the den when she arrives. I'm going up to change. And Molly, I'll want you there too, young lady. Joan, I'd like you to be there too."

Molly got an awful feeling. What had she done wrong? Dad saved "young lady" for serious occasions. When she heard the door knocker, she let Charlotte in and took her to the den where her parents were waiting.

"Molly, we have a damage control problem because of that debate you were in at Shipton Friends," her dad said.

The congressman tossed three newspapers down on the desk. One was the familiar *Spring Grove Sentinel;* the other two were daily papers from larger Texas cities. "Somehow Claytie Lawson got hold of your school newspaper. He quotes you as saying that your dad's in favor of gun control."

"It's true, isn't it, Dad?" Molly asked. "You told me yourself."

"Yes, but I didn't mean that you should

quote me in your debate. I was giving you a private opinion. You should have understood that. Members of a congressman's family have to be careful about what they say."

Dad picked up the closest newspaper. "Here's what Claytie said in his column: 'Our new congressman, Justin Spalding, is in favor of gun control, according to the *Middle School Echo.* That just happens to be the school paper of Shipton Friends School in Washington, where Molly Spalding, the congressman's daughter, is in the seventh grade.'"

Molly's father read the whole article through to the end which concluded with the comment that "No Texas congressman has ever voted in favor of a federal law regulating the sale of guns to private citizens. Let's hope Congressman Spalding won't be the first!"

"Dad, I don't know how Mr. Lawson got the school newspaper," Molly said. "I did send one copy to my friend Brooke in Spring Grove. You know Brooke, Dad. She doesn't even know what gun control is, I'll bet."

"Brooke? Is that Brooke Taylor?"

When Molly nodded yes, her father said to Charlotte, "There's the answer. Fred Taylor, Brooke's Dad, is very active in the National Rifle Association. Unfortunately, Molly, you couldn't have picked a worse place to send it." He asked his press aide, "Have you received any calls as a result of these columns?"

"No, the gun control issue doesn't seem to be hot right now, Justin. Maybe people will just forget this. I've checked, and the seven other papers that print Claytie's column didn't print it this week." Charlotte sounded optimistic.

Congressman Spalding played with a letter opener on the desk. "When I run again I'll need to have a policy ready on gun control." He was quiet a moment. He added, "Or not run again."

"Oh, Dad!" Molly thought of Vivian Keegan's father losing the election on the issue of gun control. Would she be the cause of her father's defeat?

Her mother reached out and put an arm around her. "Don't take it too hard, honey," she said. "We've always known that some day your Dad will have to tell Texans how he feels about gun control."

"Mom's right, Molly," Dad said. "Who knows? Maybe I'll be such a terrific congressman that voters will re-elect me anyway." He patted Molly on the shoulder, and she felt relieved.

The following Saturday Molly went down to Independence Avenue again to meet Kwai. She checked all the vans parked near the Air and Space Museum, and even those near the Hirshhorn Art Museum, but couldn't find Kwai's van. What could have happened?

She saw another Vietnamese family in a van selling T-shirts. She walked up to the window, and a man opened it.

"Excuse me, sir," Molly said, "I'm looking for the Vietnamese family who sells half-smokes."

"The half-smoke van. They no here, no more," the man said. He shook his head, his lower lip protruding. "They no get new license."

He slid the window closed.

Molly backed away from the van. She had lost Kwai. She didn't know Kwai's family name, and certainly not her telephone number. Kwai had said the name once, but she couldn't remember it. Now she had no way to reach her. Molly pounded determinedly on the van's window. The man looked out at her suspiciously, then opened the glass a tiny bit.

"Please, sir, I have to get in touch with the family who sells half-smokes. Maybe we can help them. My mother is a lawyer. Do you have their telephone number?" Molly was begging, trying to hold back tears.

The man looked at her uncertainly for a moment. Then he walked over to papers that were piled on the van's dashboard. After shuffling through the pile, he took a pencil from his shirt pocket and wrote some words and numbers slowly on the inside of a matchbook cover.

"Okay. That the number. He need big help," the man said briefly. Molly saw a look of concern cross his face, and she knew that he was worried about Kwai's family. She thanked him and ran most of the way home. She let herself into the house and saw that her mother was halfway up the stairs with the vacuum cleaner. Molly ran up the stairs. Her mother was startled and turned off the machine.

"Molly, is something wrong?" she asked.

"Yes, Mom, I need a lawyer," Molly said. She sat down on the stairs and told what she had heard about Kwai's family.

"I'm sorry about your friend, Molly, but I don't think I should get involved," she said. "Maybe they did something illegal to lose their license."

Mrs. Spalding sat down on the stairway. Molly didn't move.

"Mom, will you please talk to Kwai's parents? I can call her and see if they want a lawyer. They could even come here, so it's no trouble for you. They're good people, Mom."

"All right, Molly," Mom agreed. "Call your friend. If her family wants legal advice, I'll be happy to have them come here."

Molly gave her mom a quick hug, then went to the phone and pressed the numbers scribbled on the matchbook cover. The telephone rang three times and no one answered. Molly's heart sank. Maybe the family had moved. Maybe . . .

"Hello," answered a voice that sounded too timid to belong to the bright and funny Kwai that Molly knew.

"Kwai?"

"This is Kwai. Who is calling, please?"

"Kwai, it's Molly Spalding. Am I glad I found you!" Molly shouted into the phone. "I heard your father lost his license to sell food. What happened?"

"I wanted to call and tell you what happened, but I didn't have your telephone number," Kwai said. "My father sent in the money to get his vendor's license renewed, but the District of Columbia government says he can't get one. Now he might have to sell the van and find some other job. It's bad, Molly."

"Hold on," Molly said. "Ask your father if he'd like to talk to my mother. She's a lawyer. Maybe she can help."

That afternoon the silver van with the big pink half-smokes sign on its side pulled up in front of the Spaldings' house. Molly and her mother went out to the van and introduced themselves. Kwai's family name turned out to be Nguyen.

"Do come in, Mr. and Mrs. Nguyen," Mrs. Spalding said. "And Kwai, of course," she added with a smile.

After an hour of conversation with a few translations by Kwai, and tea and cookies served by Molly, the Nguyen family left. Mrs. Spalding had agreed to meet Mr. and Mrs. Nguyen on Monday morning to start working on the license renewal problem.

Molly and her mom waved good-bye to the Nguyens as the van moved up C Street. Mrs. Spalding said, "What a lovely family, Molly. I hope I can help them straighten out their licensing problem."

When Molly got home from school Monday afternoon, her mom was making Texas chili, because her dad had promised to be home for dinner. Her mother was in a happy mood, scurrying about adding finishing touches to their meal.

"Mr. Nguyen and I spent three hours going around City Hall trying to meet with officials who weren't there—at least they weren't there for us," she told Molly. "We're going back again tomorrow. Mr. Nguyen is a fine man."

She finished tossing a big salad in the glass bowl and handed it to Molly to carry to the table. "You know, I'm really enjoying helping Mr. Nguyen." She smiled. "I've missed my law practice, but I had no idea how much. Especially when I can help a

119

family like this who couldn't afford to hire a lawyer."

If anyone could help the Nguyen family, Molly thought, her mother could.

"Hi, everyone," Dad called from the hall.

"Just in time, Justin. Chili's on!" his wife answered.

Molly called Billy home from his friend Chris's house across the street, and the four of them gathered hungrily around the table.

Molly's father turned to her. "Before I forget, I have a package for you. Charlotte gave it to me as I went out the door."

He passed a big manila envelope to her.

"Thanks, Dad," Molly said, and she put the package on the floor. "I'll open it after dinner," she said.

Just then Mrs. Spalding brought a huge bowl of steaming chili to the table.

"This sure does make me think of home. Pass your plates everyone," he said, as he scooped out heaping servings for the family.

"Don't forget your package, Molly," her mother reminded her as soon as they finished their dessert. "What in the world would Charlotte be sending to you?"

"Oh, uh, just something she got me for

school," Molly answered, trying to pass it off.

"Just something?" her mother persisted. "It looks like a lot of something to me—a package that size."

Now her dad became curious too. Molly opened the package, and out fell two thick, typed reports in handsome blue folders with the seal of the Library of Congress on them.

"What's this from the Congressional Research Service?" he asked, recognizing the seal. He looked at the titles printed on the pages, picked one up, and started reading.

"Belgium Faces the Changes in the Common Market," he read out loud.

"Sweden's Political Future Looks Unclear," Mrs. Spalding read from the other one.

"My report will be on Belgium and my friend Ashley's is on Sweden. She told me if I got the people at the Library of Congress to do the research, it would save us a lot of time." Molly tried to sound calm, but her heart was racing.

Molly's mother and father looked surprised. A tense silence hung over the room. Then, without a word, both of her parents started tearing the reports into tiny pieces.

Dad's mouth was tight and his face was grim. "Molly," he said, "if you need to cheat like this to pass the seventh grade at Shipton Friends, we'll find you an easier school."

"Ashley says that all the congressmen's kids do it—for themselves and their friends. She didn't say anything about cheating."

"Not cheating?" he said, echoing Molly's words. "It is in my book, young lady. You're one congressman's daughter who isn't going to turn in a report written by some Ph.D. in the Congressional Research Service. And who, may I ask, is Ashley?" To Molly, Dad sounded demanding, like a lawyer cross-examining a witness in a trial.

"She's the only friend I have in that dumb school. But that's okay, because if I don't have a report about a country, I'm going to flunk out anyway!" Molly shouted.

She got up from her chair, ran upstairs to her room and slammed the door. Then she flopped down on her bed and pulled a pillow over her head.

Molly had never felt so miserable. Deep down she had thought it must be wrong to have a researcher in the Library of Congress write her report, but Ashley had said all the congressmen's kids did it.

If she were speaking to Mark these days, she'd ask him if he got help from the Library of Congress. Or if she had known Jocelyn better she'd have called her. The way Ashley talked, it was acceptable for the kids at school to have reports written for them. Now she had only two weeks left until she had to give her report. Worse than that, tomorrow she had to tell Ashley what happened to the reports.

As Molly was thinking about what she'd say to Ashley, she heard a knock on the door.

"Is now a good time to talk?" It was Mom.

"Okay," Molly answered weakly.

Mom opened the door, walked across the room and sat on a corner of Molly's bed.

"Molly, your Dad and I want the best for you," Mom said slowly. "But having reports written for you is cheating, even if you change some of the words. We know you can do well at Shipton on your own. All we ask is that you do your best—on your own."

Then Mom bent over, raised the pillow from Molly's face and kissed her on her forehead. "I love you, Molly. Good night."

When Molly woke up the next morning, she thought that if she concentrated very hard, she might be sick. She felt around her middle, hoping for appendicitis or even stomach flu, but she couldn't stir up the tiniest ache or pain. She sniffed a few times, but she couldn't even pretend to have cold.

Molly sighed and got out of bed. There was no escape. She was completely healthy, and she had to go to school and face Ashley with the bad news.

At the subway station Molly looked around, trying not to be obvious, but didn't see Mark. She missed his company on the way to school these days, but since the big debate she still hadn't spoken to him. Now she realized that he had given better arguments, but she still felt he shouldn't have called her his opponent. And how could he be so blind about the dangers of hand guns, especially living here in Washington?

At school, Molly's day was crammed with special things Mrs. Gale and Mrs. Miller dreamed up for her, and she didn't have a minute to talk to Ashley until after school.

As her friend started up the aisle with her backpack, Molly called out to her. "I have some bad news, Ashley," she said. "My father and mother tore up the reports the Library of Congress wrote for us. They say it's cheating. So I'm sorry," Molly said weakly.

"Why did you tell your father?" Ashley demanded. "He didn't need to know."

"His press aide gave him the reports to carry home to me."

"I was counting on getting an A, the way I did when Vivian lived here. Thanks for nothing, Molly."

"I've been thinking about it, Ashley. It really would be cheating to use those reports," Molly said quietly.

"You sure are a goody-goody," Ashley said. "You'd better realize that you're in the big leagues now. It's dog-eat-dog in this school."

Ashley gave Molly a sly grin as a new thought struck her. "You'll probably flunk social studies if you try to write a report on your own. Mr. Wolff grades really hard."

Tears stung Molly's eyes. What a friend Ashley turned out to be! She was just using me, Molly realized, because I'm a congressman's daughter.

Molly felt completely alone. She and Mark weren't speaking, Kwai was way over in Arlington, and Ashley was no friend. And to make matters worse, Molly knew nothing about Belgium.

# Ten

MOLLY opened the front door on Saturday morning, and it was a rare, glorious spring day. Molly stood on the steps and watched Billy as he went off to yet another birthday party in the neighborhood. She had wrapped his present in red-and-white striped paper, with two balloons attached. Billy disappeared around the corner to his friend Todd's house, trailing the red balloons behind him.

She knew Kwai wouldn't be on the Mall in the van today because her mother was still trying to get the Nguyens' license renewed. In an hour Molly had to go to the library and begin her research on Belgium, but right now she was going to take a few minutes for her first bicycle ride of spring. She got her bike out of the garage where it had been parked since the move.

"I'm going off for a ride, Mom," she called. Her mother was busy with a trowel working in the flower garden. "I may go down by the Smithsonian museums."

"Okay, but watch out for traffic. Remember, this isn't Spring Grove!" her mom called out as Molly headed out.

As if I need to be reminded, Molly thought.

She rode down the street, happy to be back on her beloved blue and white bike after too many months. She tingled with that special feeling of freedom that her bicycle gave her. It ran down her spine and then down her legs. She breathed deeply. She had almost forgotten that wonderful feeling during the cold Washington winter.

On her bike, Molly felt like an uncaged bird, free to come and go as she pleased. She might even get a little lost for a while, but she didn't care. She squeezed her hand brakes, testing them as she rode down a small hill to see that they were in order.

First she rode to the Capitol—quiet this

Saturday morning—its parking lot almost empty. She zigzagged in and out of it, and slowed down as she recognized Officer Knott, her policeman friend from Amarillo, who was giving directions to a group of tourists.

In front of the Capitol steps Molly tried riding "no hands" for a distance to see if she could still do it in spite of the long winter with no practice. She heard applause behind her and turned to look back.

Mark was there, sitting on a bike, clapping his hands loudly.

"Very good, Molly, I'm impressed. Getting ready to ride in the circus?"

"Sure. As soon as I perfect my handstand on the handlebars."

Molly knew she'd broken her promise to herself never to speak to Mark again, but she couldn't help it. He was being so friendly she had to answer. She saw his gleaming red and silver bicycle was brand new, with trail-type tires, lots of gears, and fancy handlebars.

"Got a new bike, Mark?" Molly asked. And when he nodded, she said, "It's a beauty."

"Thanks. It's pretty fancy compared to the old one I inherited from my big brother." He rubbed an imaginary bit of dust off the handlebars. "This was an 'instead-of' present today."

"Instead of what?"

"Instead of having a party. It's my birthday, but my dad's so busy at the Capitol. Now that he's a committee chairman he doesn't have time to do anything with me. He and Mom asked if I'd like a new bike for my birthday instead of having kids over for a party."

"Maybe I'll try that next time," Molly said thoughtfully. She didn't have enough friends for a party anyway.

Molly continued. "I can almost count on one hand how many times my dad has been home for dinner since we got here in January. In Spring Grove we had a family rule that Dad made pancakes and sausage for us on Saturday morning. It's only happened twice in Washington. Happy birthday, Mark."

She got on her bike and pedaled away.

"Wait up, Molly!" Mark called, catching up to her. "I know you were mad at me about our gun control debate. I shouldn't have blasted you and used those slogans. I'm so used to arguing politics with my big brothers that I never take it personally. I get bullheaded when I'm debating without even thinking about it."

"I was in over my head," Molly admitted. "I've never even seen a real debate." She shook her head, remembering, then smiled. "You certainly converted the class to being against gun control."

He grinned. "It was kind of fun in a Quaker school to defend guns when Quakers don't believe in any kind of violence. I love to argue. Next year in the eighth grade I can go out for the debate team. I can hardly wait."

"Oh, I'll want to do that, too," Molly said at once. Then she remembered that she might not even get out of the seventh grade.

Mark leaned over his handlebars. "One more thing. If you want to know the truth, I'm in favor of gun control, too. But my brother told me that in a debate it's easier to argue against something than in favor of it. It always is."

Molly could hardly believe her ears.

Suddenly she felt that a great cloud had been lifted. Mark had been her first friend here, and she didn't want to lose his friendship over gun control.

"Ashley told me you got your debate information from the Congressional Research Service. You really had a lot of facts," Molly said innocently. She wondered what he'd say.

Mark reacted as if he had been bitten by a snake. "Ashley WHAT?" he all but yelled. "She's wrong, let me tell you. Didn't you read your copy of the student handbook? Shipton has an honor code, and everyone knows all about the Congressional Research Service. Getting a report already written by someone at the Library of Congress would be the fastest way to get expelled from Shipton."

Molly confessed to Mark that she hadn't read the handbook. She also told him about what Ashley had said, that all the congressmen's kids used the research service.

"You know what?" Mark said. "I think Ashley lied when she said Vivian Keegan got reports for her. I've known Vivian since pre-kindergarten days, and she's no cheater. I think Ashley was just trying to make you think that everybody does it."

"Now I have to go to the library and find out about Belgium by myself," Molly said.

Mark smiled. "And I'm going to the Tidal Basin to see if any of the cherry trees are in bloom. I can ride under the cherry trees for two miles around the Tidal Basin."

"Oh, I've never been there," Molly said, "but today the library's open, so I'd better go."

"How about tomorrow afternoon?" Mark asked. "You can't work all the time, and the library's closed on Sunday anyway."

"That would be super, Mark. Two o'clock, okay?"

"Great. I'll ride by your house then, Molly."

"Happy birthday, Mark," Molly smiled and waved. They were friends again, and she felt good about that. She had been so lonely not speaking to him. That was all over now.

While she was attaching her bicycle lock at the library's bike rack, Molly got an idea. She didn't know anything about Belgians, but because of her friendship with Kwai and the Nguyen family, she was learning more and more each day about how the Vietnamese live. Why not do a report on Vietnam?

In the library she settled down at a table, opened her notebook and found the list of countries. No check mark appeared next to Vietnam. Molly could have it if Mr. Wolff approved. She sighed. She would simply have to take a chance that he would let her change her topic at this late date.

She walked determinedly to the reference librarian and said, "I'm giving a fifteen-minute talk on Vietnam. Will you please help me find information about that country?"

She read and wrote until the library closed at five o'clock.

\* \* \* \* \*

On Monday night, Mrs. Spalding plopped a huge pizza with sausage, mushrooms, green peppers, and extra cheese down in the middle of the dining room table.

"This is dinner, folks," she said. "Sorry, Justin, I know it's not as fancy as what you get in the House dining room, but it's been a wild day. I stopped on the way home from City Hall and bought the biggest pizza I could find."

"My favorite food," Billy declared eagerly.

"Mr. Congressman, will you please carve?" asked Mom, passing the pizza cutter to her husband while she served a tossed salad.

"I have some good news to report," Mom said with a jaunty air. "Today Mr. Nguyen and I and about fifty people in City Hall finally solved the great license mystery. It turns out that there are two Li M. Nguyens with a vendor's license in the District of Columbia."

"You mean that's a common name?"

"As common in Vietnam as Smith or Jones is here, he told me. The other Li M. Nguyen had a bad record, and every time we applied for the license, the other man's record came up on the computer and rejected our application."

She took a bite of her piece of pizza and then continued. "Today our Mr. Nguyen was fingerprinted and proved he wasn't the other man with the record. Our friend had to rush off to his temporary job, so I stayed and got the license for him."

She turned to Molly. "Hon, I thought you and I might take it over to their apartment in Arlington after dinner, if you don't have too much homework."

"Let's all go," Dad suggested. "I'd like to meet this family I've heard so much about. I don't even have to go back to the House tonight."

"Do you know, Justin," Mrs. Spalding said, "it really felt good to help out the Nguyens. I don't know when I've enjoyed something so much." She was quiet for a moment, then said, "One thing I've learned is that it's time for me to get my license to practice law in the District of Columbia." She picked up another piece of the huge pizza. "Molly and Billy are pretty well adjusted to life in the big city. And frankly, I miss my law practice."

"I understand, Joan," Dad said. "And I'm happy for you."

"I want to work to help refugees like Mr. Nguyen who can't afford these big city lawyers," Mom said.

"You could set up an office in that empty room downstairs," her husband suggested.

"It has its own entrance, and you'd still be close by for the kids."

After supper the four Spaldings drove across the Potomac River to Arlington to find the Nguyens' apartment. At an old red brick building they walked up three flights of stairs and down a long, dark hall.

Mom rang the bell at apartment 336. Kwai's father opened the door hesitantly. Molly thought he looked a little surprised to see all the Spaldings there. Then he opened the door wide.

"Come in, come in," he urged, smiling and bowing.

Too eager to wait, Mrs. Spalding stepped forward and handed a big, brown envelope to him with a grand gesture. "At last, Mr. Nguyen!" she said triumphantly. "Here's your new license."

Mr. Nguyen looked at it, not quite believing, his hands shaking as he read the English slowly. Abruptly he turned and shouted in Vietnamese. Kwai and her mother came running from behind closed curtains in the back of the apartment. Kwai's mother started to cry, she was so happy. Everyone was introduced to everyone else.

"Mr. Spalding, your wife, she work very, very hard to help me," Mr. Nguyen said, continuing to shake Molly's father's hand. The short Vietnamese man looked up at the tall congressman. "You a lawyer, too?"

"I used to be," the congressman said with a smile, "but now I'm—I work for the government."

Molly and Billy exchanged glances.

Good ol' Dad, Molly thought. He didn't want to take away Mom's moment of glory by saying that he was a congressman.

The Spaldings drank the tea and soft drinks that the Nguyens offered. Before saying good-bye, Molly said she did have one favor to ask of Kwai.

"A week from tomorrow I have to give a fifteen-minute report on Vietnam. Will you tell me some things about it?"

"Sure. When do we start?" Kwai asked.

\* \* \* \* \* \*

At exactly 11:05 on the morning of March 29, Molly came into Mr. Wolff's room from the girls' locker room, where she had gone to change. It was her turn to report on

138

a country. She was wearing the blue satin dress and trousers that Kwai had worn for the Tet celebration. Her friend's gold crown sat on her head.

"Good morning," she said to the startled class. "I am wearing a traditional Vietnamese outfit for Tet—that's Vietnam's New Year's celebration. I am going to tell you about the country of Vietnam and the Vietnamese people.

"People in Washington think of my country when they see the Vietnam War Memorial, one of the most popular monuments in the city. It is visited every day by relatives and friends of the more than 55,000 Americans who died in the Vietnamese conflict. Living in this area are more than 100,000 refugees from Vietnam, people who came to this country after that war ended. Most of them have already become United States citizens. Now let me tell you about Vietnam, as it used to be and as it is today."

Molly opened her black notebook. She read some of the information from her notes and told the rest from memory. She was careful not to speak too fast because she knew her report must last the assigned fifteen minutes.

First she told about her costume and the celebration of Tet. Then she described the country's geography and explained some of its history, including the most current information she had read in news magazines.

Molly looked up at the clock—fourteen minutes. She had one minute to go.

"My friend, who was born in Vietnam, will now perform a dance the Vietnamese people perform to celebrate the festival of Tet."

She put a tape in the tape player on Mr. Wolff's desk. Strange music with twangy sounds and the clang of cymbals filled the air. Molly walked to the door and turned the knob, hoping that her mom had brought Kwai to Shipton on time.

She opened the door and in danced Kwai wearing a pink satin Vietnamese dress over white satin trousers. As the door closed behind her, Molly caught a glimpse of her mother in the hall smiling.

Kwai danced about the room. Waving a branch of yellow forsythia blossoms, she moved gracefully to the strange music. When it ended, the class clapped loudly. Kwai bowed modestly.

"Kwai, could you please introduce yourself in Vietnamese?" Molly asked.

Kwai responded in Vietnamese.

"Can you please say good-bye to the students?"

Again Kwai responded in Vietnamese, bowed again, and danced out the door. The class applauded enthusiastically.

Mr. Wolff stood up in the back of the room. "Molly, please call your friend back. You've gone over fifteen minutes, but I think the class would like to hear an explanation of the dance."

Molly opened the door again and motioned to Kwai, who was waiting outside.

"Kwai, will you please tell the class about your dance?"

Kwai faced the class and smiled. "Good morning, everyone," she said in English. I'm Kwai Nguyen, and I'm in the seventh grade in Arlington. I got excused to come here to dance for Molly's report because she is my very good friend. Let me tell you something about Tet and the dance I just did."

After Kwai's explanation, applause followed as Kwai and Molly walked out of the room. The dreaded report was over at last, Molly realized. Her knees still felt a little weak. Her talk had gone well, and Kwai had delighted the class.

The next morning Molly went to her homeroom after Meeting, where Mrs. Gale waited for her.

"I have some good news!" Mrs. Gale said, smiling. "Mr. Chipman just told me that you have completed all the requirements for algebra and English and will no longer need tutoring. Now you'll be able to join your friends for lunch at noon, and you'll be free to go out for soccer or field hockey or tennis or chorus or drama or anything else after school you'd like to do. Mrs. Miller says that you've worked hard, Molly, and I'm happy to hear it. I know it wasn't easy."

It was awful, Molly thought. But now it's over. I'm here for keeps.

When the last morning class was dismissed for lunch, Molly walked out of the room and started in the direction of the lunchroom. It felt a little like her first day of school again, when she didn't know anybody. She had gotten used to eating with Mrs. Miller and now she wouldn't have her company any longer.

Molly walked hesitantly into the lunchroom, wondering how she would be accepted at her table. She saw a raised arm waving to her from the other side of the room. Jocelyn was sitting at the table with several students, but determinedly saving a space next to her. Jocelyn smiled, nodded, and motioned to Molly to join her.

Molly waved back and started across the room. Suddenly she knew that everything was going to be just fine.

# About the Author

Living in the middle of political life in Washington has given Patricia Maloney Markun a close look at the happiness and the pains, the wins and the losses of the families of our nation's members of Congress. *The Congressman's Daughter* is based on the lives of a number of senators and representatives who have been her friends, some of them neighbors on her quiet Washington street. She also drew on her two sons' experience at Sidwell Friends School, a Quaker school in Washington similar to the school Molly attends in the book.

The story takes place on Capitol Hill, the part of the city that surrounds the Capitol itself, and where many members of Congress and their families live. Mrs. Markun likes to bicycle on Capitol Hill, where a demonstration, a political gathering, or even senators and Supreme Court justices walking by makes a bicycle ride interesting.

Patricia Markun started writing when she was very young. At the age of 11, she won first prize in a story competition sponsored by the *Duluth Herald* newspaper. When she saw her story in print, she decided to be a writer when she grew up. Several years later, she graduated from the School of Journalism at the University of Minnesota.

Her favorite places to write are on a train going on a long trip or in an isolated mountain cabin.